THE Dubious PRANKS OF Shaindy Goodman

This is an Arthur A. Levine book
Published by Levine Querido

LQ

LEVINE QUERIDO

www.levinequerido.com • info@levinequerido.com

Levine Querido is distributed by Chronicle Books

Library of Congress Control Number: 2023931661

ISBN 9781646142644

Printed in China

Published November 2023
First Printing

The text type was set in Centaur

THE Dubious PRANKS OF Shaindy Goodman

Mari Lowe

LQ

Montclair | Amsterdam | Hoboken

For Batsheva, my partner in surviving sixth grade,
And for all the readers still muddling through it.

גם זה יעבור .

CHAPTER 1

The lights next door are flickering, casting moving shadows on the stillness of my backyard while I try to stand on shaky Rollerblades. I know that it's not a storm that's interfering with the lights. It's clear outside, and I can see all the stars from here. No, it's probably Gayil and her sisters and brothers having a dance party. I saw the packaging for a disco ball poking out of their recycling garbage can yesterday morning when I left for school, and I always hear them playing old Miami Boys Choir songs at night on top volume.

It's quiet in my house. I have one sister, not five, and Bayla is four years older than me and generally considers me a *pain in the neck*, as she complains to Ema when I'm around. We've never had a dance party, and if I put on music in our room, she tells me to stop because she's studying. Tonight, I haven't even tried. Instead, I'm doing something new.

Everyone rollerblades now. Fairview is basically built for it, with all our quiet developments and wide sidewalks. On Shabbos, the streets are empty except for the mail trucks, and little kids ride plastic bikes up and down them for the whole afternoon with no supervision. I see Gayil and Devorah and Rena skate to school every morning with their brand-name Heelys, speeding past me and weaving between minivans picking up their morning carpools.

I've never been great with Rollerblades. I like my feet planted on solid ground, thank you *very* much. I've tottered around on ice skates and held on to the wall the entire time, and I've always been shaky on a bike too. But I came back from summer camp and discovered that every sixth grader at Fairview Bais Yaakov rollerblades now except for me. I don't know when it happened or how, but I'm the last to figure it out. Again.

So now I have to get good at rollerblading overnight, and I dug Bayla's old Rollerblades out of the closet and forced them onto my too-wide feet. I clomp around our flat wooden patio in them, wishing that I had some of those Heelys that Gayil wears. They're just regular sneakers with wheels that snap out of the soles, and I had begged my mother for my own pair earlier this week.

I'm not spending that much on a pair of shoes you aren't going to wear, Ema had said, and I'm determined to show her that I can do it and earn those Heelys. Except the rollerblading isn't going that well. My legs split and my knees bend and I'm falling off the patio and onto the grass, my arm slamming into a clod of dirt that feels suspiciously wet.

"Ow! Ugh." I try to wipe my arm off on the edge of the patio and succeed only in smearing it around my arm even more. "Oh, *gross.* This better not be cat poop." We feed the local cats and they like to hang out in the backyard, wandering down the strip of grass that we share with a dozen other neighbors along the street. Gayil always shrieks and runs when she sees them, but I like the cats. Except *this,* if it's what I'm afraid it is.

I hobble to the back door in my Rollerblades and push it open with my clean arm, wiggling out of the Rollerblades and going to wash up. Maybe I'll practice more tomorrow morning before school. I can't stand the thought of another morning going by, walking with my head down into the school building as other girls zip by on their skates. *Chubby Shaindy just isn't athletic enough for Rollerblades*, I imagine them thinking. *Awkward Shaindy doesn't even know that everyone has Heelys now.*

No one is mean to me aloud, of course. We're one of those classes that everyone likes to talk about, a model Bais Yaakov class that is so *sweet* and *bright* and *respectful* that every teacher looks forward to having us. But I've never really fit in with everyone else. I'm the girl who waits on the side when we do group projects, hoping someone will invite me into their group before the teacher has to assign them to me. I follow other girls around at recess, trying to join their conversations and always falling flat. I just don't have the kind of magic that Gayil has, that energy that makes everyone want to be her friend.

Maybe it's not worth it, learning how to rollerblade. By the time I get my Heelys, everyone else will be done with them and I'll be the one who caught on too late.

I head up the stairs to my room, getting an irritated "Can you not stomp so loud?" from Bayla at the desk before I dump the Rollerblades in the closet again and climb up onto my top bunk to read a book. I'd rather read than rollerblade anyway.

Still, I peer out my window, wondering if I might be able to see the Itzhaki girls dancing next door. My window looks directly at Gayil's, and I figure that the disco ball must be set up there.

But it isn't. The flashing lights are coming from downstairs, and Gayil's room is dimly lit, only a lamp near the window illuminating it. Gayil is standing in her room, staring out the window with distant eyes.

She doesn't see me at first, because I'm near the top of the window, stretched over the side of the bunk bed to see out of it. Then, she must have noticed the movement, because her eyes flicker up and catch mine.

They hold my gaze, and there is something strange glittering in them that I don't understand. I lift a hand and wave to her, half-hearted, because I know that I'll just get a strained smile and a little wave in response from someone who doesn't want to be around me.

But I don't. Gayil crooks a finger as though she is beckoning me, and I blink at her in surprise. It must be a mistake. Maybe I'd misread what she was doing. I pull back, baffled, and Bayla says from the desk, "Can you stop that thumping? This Ramban is *killing* me."

"Study somewhere else, then," I say, climbing down the ladder of the bunk bed just to annoy her. I peek back at the window, and I jump, startled. Gayil is still standing there, frozen in place like a picture. Her brown eyes look almost golden in the lamp's light, and her light brown skin is shadowed.

Carefully, I walk across the room, a cool breeze wafting in from outside and tingling at my skin. I close the window where it's cracked open, an excuse to walk over to it, and I feel the steadying sensation of the hard plastic under my fingers, the faint smell of the fresh yellow paint by the wall. I dare to look up again.

Gayil is still there, a smile on her face. It's almost teasing, almost coy, transforming her face into something mischievous. I pause, transfixed, and I know that she can see me staring at her. She lifts her hands, and I see that there's a paper in them, words written in stark black marker against the white background.

The sign says, *WANT TO KNOW A SECRET?*

Gayil raises her eyebrows invitingly, and I am helpless to do anything but nod.

CHAPTER 2

Our backyards are all connected. There's one neighbor who had enclosed his, had broken the river of grass that stretches down the block, but the rest of them are free for all of us. In the development where we live, most families have at least five or six kids and two families live in each house, and the kids rule the neighborhood. I've been walking to school alone since I was seven, alongside a crowd of other girls and boys heading in the same direction.

There's a big trampoline behind Gayil's house where my classmates hang out after school some days, and I know that Gayil will be waiting there. Carefully, I head downstairs. I have to dodge Abba where he's learning gemara in the kitchen as he eats soup, a bit of it dripped onto his red-brown beard. His shoulders are stooped from years of sitting in front of his gemara and his tortoiseshell glasses are caught between two fingers, but he straightens to smile up at me. Ema is entertaining our basement neighbor in the living room. Ema's chubby like me, but it makes her look warm and friendly instead of awkward, and her dark hair peeks out past the purple-hued headscarf that she wears on her head. She doesn't glance at me, but she knows I'm there, because she calls out, "Don't be out too late," as I pass her. "It's a school night."

I duck out the back door. Ema never has to worry about me being home on school nights—I'm not exactly a social butterfly—and I'm not going far.

The trampoline is near the back of the fence that closes off our development from the one being built behind it. One of the neighbors has put a flower bed near the trampoline, the colors dim in the dark but the scent lingers in the air. I can see an unmoving crane just past the fence, towering over the trampoline and casting a triangular shadow across me. Gayil is sitting at the side of the trampoline beneath the crane, long legs splayed out in front of her, and I climb up the ladder into the trampoline, bouncing a little as I crawl across the mat to her.

Gayil doesn't look at me. She's staring at something in her hand, and I squint at it in the dim light in the backyard. I can just make out a rectangular shape, hard plastic that looks vaguely familiar. I edge down along the trampoline beside her, the hard plastic textured enough that I can feel it on my knees through my grey pleated skirt, and I venture, "Did you want me to come out here?"

Gayil startles, lurching back on the bouncy mat. "Oh," she says, and she brightens, straightening out her own skirt over her knees. She's already changed from her uniform skirt to a trendier black one. She grins at me, white teeth gleaming beneath her braces. I've never seen her look so excited to see me. "Shaindy. There you are. What took you so long?"

It's been five minutes. I blink at her. She says, "Never mind. I have the *wildest* thing to show you. I found it right outside the school building—just lying there yesterday—and I was popping the wheel out of my Heelys when I spotted it. One of them has a stuck heel, right here, see?" She sticks her shoe out to show me, and I watch, baffled at what I'm doing out here.

Gayil and I aren't friends. When she first moved in next door, our parents set up a few playdates. We were five, and we were about to start in the same school, so it seemed a no-brainer that we would become best friends. But I was a shy kid, and I guess Gayil lost interest during those first few playdates. Within a few weeks, we'd started school and Gayil had immediately drawn in the rest of the class while I'd lurked in corners and watched. I never quite caught up with everyone else.

It's not like we hate each other—our class is too *nice* for that—but Gayil has never shown much interest in hanging out with me. This feels like a sudden, precious moment, a turning point for me. Either that, or there's been a horrible mistake.

I say, "There's a Thumbtack jammed into the pocket where the wheel slides in. That's why it isn't popping out easily." I can see it glinting in the light of the Itzhaki patio lamp, silver against the smooth red-and-blue of the wheel.

"Whoa, really?" Gayil blinks at me, then pulls off the shoe and tugs out the tack. She tosses it carelessly over the net of the trampoline, into the high grass that crawls up the fence on our side, and then tries popping the wheel in and out again. "Genius," she says, grinning, and my cheeks warm. "*Anyway.* I saw this then." She sticks out her hand and opens her palm, and I see that hard plastic rectangle in it. It's a bright teal, flat and thick, and it isn't labeled, but I know exactly what it is. I've seen teachers use them for years outside the big grey-brick building where I spend most of my waking hours.

It's a key fob, one that only faculty has, and it's the key to enter the school building. There's security too, and they'll buzz people in most of the time. But the fob is for after hours, for late evening events and early arrivals, and every teacher has one.

"Is it Morah Neuman's?" I wonder, going through the number of teachers who might be near our classroom. "Or Mrs. Beim? There's also Morah Adelman next door, and Mrs. Gelman is always forgetting her bag everywhere so it might be—"

"Shaindy," Gayil says, cutting me off, and I stop before I can embarrass myself again. I think quickly, hesitate, and run through the possibilities. Gayil isn't bringing me here because of something she can fix by bringing the fob to the school office. She hadn't brought me here just to share either. I'm not her *confidante*.

Which means . . . "You want to use it, don't you?" I breathe, a breeze tickling at my hair as I stare at the fob. "What are you planning? Some kind of . . . like, a school spirit thing?" It's under a week until Rosh Hashanah, the Jewish New Year, and maybe Gayil is organizing a surprise for the class before it starts. Gayil does stuff like that all the time, little projects to make the class excited or to help a teacher out. She's the *perfect Bais Yaakov girl*, one of our teachers had said last year, and we'd all laughed and known it was true. The perfect Bais Yaakov girl is an elusive concept, someone respectful and understanding and energetic and modest, friends with everyone and giving of her time, and Gayil is as close as it gets. She dresses the part too, straight hair pulled back with a headband at all times and her uniform fitted so it's clean looking and flat without being too tight. Even her nonuniform skirt makes her look more like one of our younger teachers, mature and graceful, and I could see Gayil arranging something that the teachers would have done otherwise.

Gayil laughs. "No," she says, and there is a strange note to her voice, a shift that is mischievous and secretive at once. "Nothing like that. I thought we might do a few pranks."

"Pranks?" I echo, baffled. I don't know Gayil well, but none of what I do know about her really fits with this image. "Like practical jokes? On the teachers?"

"No way," Gayil says, horrified. "Not on *teachers*. That would be so disrespectful." She shrugs. "I don't know. It's been a rough start to the year, right? Sixth grade is *hard*."

I nod in bewildered agreement. Sixth grade *is* hard. There are suddenly six teachers—two for Hebrew subjects and four for English—and they all have different rules, different schedules, different homework. It feels like there's a test every day, and I'm always scrambling for the right notebook or binder. It's a lot of work, but people like Gayil always sail through it.

Maybe I've overestimated Gayil. Maybe Gayil is just as lost as I am. "This could be a fun distraction," she says. "A mystery that no one else will be able to solve. I bet it'll make everyone a little less stressed." She grins. "I think we should start with Rena Pollack. She could use a laugh."

Rena Pollack is one of Gayil's closest best friends, a tall girl with curly dark ringlets that are always held back in a headband, neat and modest, just like our teachers want our hair to be. In summer camp, she used to bring a stack of hair products to the shower, each one carefully applied. I sit behind her in math class and spend a good portion of every period imagining how those ringlets would spring back into place if I tugged them. If Gayil is starting with Rena, then this is harmless, a little bit of fun between friends.

I've been invited along because I'm *not* a friend, I realize suddenly. I'm the outsider who would never be targeted in something like this. My classmates are too nice to be bullies, and this would feel too much like bullying if I were the one who had the practical jokes played on her.

But I've never gotten a chance like this. Once, back in summer camp, I'd been the one with the plan that the other Fairview girls had followed enthusiastically, but that had been because Gayil had disappeared for a little while. I'm not a leader, and I'm not the girl who anyone picks to be their coconspirator. This is a chance to be like *Gayil*, to spend time with the most popular girl in school, and it sounds like it's going to be exciting too.

I don't think twice about it. "And you want me to come with you?" I blurt out, still unsure about it. "Not one of your friends?"

Gayil scoffs. "They can't keep a secret," she says, tossing her gleaming black hair. "They'll start giggling about it the minute that Rena finds out what we have in store for her. You though . . ." She pokes a finger at my face, prodding my forehead, and she tilts her head and takes me in. "I have no idea what's going on in that head of yours," she says thoughtfully. "I bet you're good at secrets."

She clambers to her feet, popping out the wheels of her shoes and gliding across the trampoline mat. "Come on," she says cheerfully. "Are you in?"

I follow behind her, bouncing once to throw myself to the middle of the trampoline, and once more to land near the ladder. Gayil watches me, eyebrows raised, and I say, "Yeah," trying to seem cool and disinterested. "I'm in."

Inside, I'm on top of the world.

CHAPTER 3

Fairview is one of the most Jewish towns in the whole United States. When my parents had been kids, it had been a small town that had been maybe half Jewish. Now, it's huge. All those kids had grown up and had their own kids, and there had been no more space in the town, just lots of empty land around it to develop into more neighborhoods. My neighborhood isn't far from a highway, but you wouldn't know it from the quiet streets and picture-perfect developments. Ours is three blocks long: a U-shaped turn with about fifty identical houses, each one with a separate apartment in the basement, and five hundred people living here in all. Twelve of them are classmates at Bais Yaakov, but only Gayil and I live on our block, the center of the U.

It's night, but the sky is cloudy and the streetlamps are bright, and the block is as alive now as if it were the afternoon. At night, there are fewer kids on toddler bikes and scooters, and more teenagers, just home from school, sitting together on benches or wandering the block. A group of high schoolers sit in the little playground at the center of the U, across from our block and next to one of the seven shuls in the development, their legs dangling down from the top of the play structure. Cars inch slowly down the street, weaving carefully between groups of kids to get to their houses.

We stay out of the street, wandering down the sidewalk like we're just another pair of friends walking together at night. "It's already getting cold and we're barely halfway through September," Gayil says, shivering. "I can't stand the cold."

"I hate when it gets dark early," I offer. "Walking home from school when it's already night is the *worst*."

"Mm," Gayil says, then, wistfully, "I miss the sun."

I venture a memory from camp. "You really loved lying in the grass during sports," I say. There had been seven of us from Fairview Bais Yaakov in our bunk, and Gayil had been the star, of course. Our counselors had loved her, and she'd been effortless in sports, had gotten the solo in the camp play, and had led the bunk everywhere. My parents had sent me to sleepaway camp in the mountains in an attempt to help me make friends, but I had remained in Gayil's shadow along with everyone else.

Gayil looks startled. "You were in Camp Kinor with us? Oh, right," she says abruptly, smiling as though she'd remembered all along. I burn with sudden humiliation, wincing at how easily I'd gone unnoticed. "The sun is so *nice* in the mountains. And the stars! Rena and I went out when there were supposed to be shooting stars and it was . . . *amazing*," she says dreamily. "I wouldn't mind nighttime if I could see that kind of show every night."

We are nearing the edge of the development, and Gayil suddenly lifts a foot and glides, her Heelys carrying her away from me. I have to run to keep up, breathing hard behind her as I follow her around the corner.

There are three schools on the next few blocks outside the development, two of them back-to-back on the same square four-street block. Down the block and on the street behind it is the other one, but it's a high school yeshiva for boys and boasts a full campus. Most of the younger boys in my development go to an elementary school across Fairview, and I like to watch them spill out of the buses when they pull up, hordes of little boys in white shirts and black pants scattering to each of the houses on the block.

The girls are divided between the two schools. Most of us go to the other two, and Fairview Bais Yaakov is the one that faces us, just across the street. It's made of grey brick, sleek and squat, and it has only two floors. The sixth grade is near the back of the second floor, and Gayil pops in the wheels on her shoes and leads me around the street, her eyes fixed on the door outside the playground. "There are cameras on the others," she says. "I checked. But the playground door doesn't have security cameras because you can only get in from inside the playground. And the playground door only opens from the inside. See?"

She gestures at the gate around the playground, but I can answer this one. Bayla and I used to go to the Bais Yaakov playground all the time on Shabbos when we were younger, just like everyone else does. "You can just stick your hand through the iron pickets of the gate, then press the push bar that's locking it. It's easy."

"Bingo." Gayil crosses the street, and I follow after her. In contrast to our bustling development, the street outside of the school is silent. At the yeshiva, there are still some men and boys lingering at the corner closest to us, waiting for rides or finishing up inside, but our school is empty. There is no security, no one to yell at us when Gayil sticks her hand through the black playground gate and pops the door open, and no one seems to notice two girls slipping into the playground together, stealing across soft rubber tiles and climbing the stairs up to the door into the school.

"Do you think the fob will work for this door?" I whisper. I can already imagine it—a failed attempt, a reported missing fob that has made the school reprogram their security system. The big silver square under the doorknob seems almost to be mocking me, reminding me exactly who I am. *You have no place here with Gayil Itzhaki,* it says, the indicator light blank. *This is just a silly, half-baked plan.*

But Gayil takes out the fob and presses it firmly against the silver square. "Let's see," she says in a murmur, and the indicator flashes green. She shoots me a smile bright enough to light up the dim playground, and she says, "We're in."

Here, she doesn't pop out the wheels of her Heelys. She walks carefully, tentatively through the hallways, and I glance around for cameras as I close the door behind us. There are none. No one can see what happens next.

We hurry past brightly decorated bulletin boards that the first-graders have decorated. *Dip the Tapuach in the Devash!* proclaims one board, each girl's face on a little red apple and the apples swimming in a sea of honey. The next one is a list of New Year's resolutions for Rosh Hashanah. A girl named Fraidel Sender has written, *For Rosh Hashanah, I am going to try to be a lawnmower.* I laugh.

Gayil is less amused. "Hurry up," she says. "No one can realize we're gone." Her voice is commanding, and I trail after her, back on track to the staircase.

The sixth-grade classrooms are in the back of the school, right over the playground. We emerge from the staircase right across from our classroom, and I hesitate again then, unsure of what comes next.

"We aren't . . . what exactly are we doing to Rena's things?" I finally think to ask.

Gayil grins. "Not her *things*. Just one thing." She digs into her sweatshirt pocket, the sleek black velour concealing any lumps in it, and she emerges with a little plastic container. "We're going to slime her hairbrush."

I wrinkle my nose. "*Ew,*" I say. Slime has always disgusted me, even when it had been a wild craze in the school. I don't like the texture, and I don't like the cool, wet feeling after letting go of it. Bais Yaakov had banned it years ago.

Gayil looks at me in disbelief. "Come on, Shaindy. Everyone likes slime. Rena *loves* slime. This is hers. She left it at my house last week." She pats the container and turns her attention to the row of lockers next to our classroom door. "Her locker is right next to yours, right?"

"Yeah. Rena Pollack, Shaindy Goodman." I point at my locker, which is unlocked. Rena's has a big pink lock on it with a glittering flower sticker on that. She forgot her combination on the second day of school, and the custodian had to snap it open. This is the replacement lock. "Do you know her combination?"

"Of *course*. She's my best friend." Gayil sounds very smug. She marches forward and puts in a combination, and the lock snaps open. "See?"

I peer in. We're barely two weeks into school, and Rena's locker is already filthy. Snack wrappers are everywhere, and loose papers poke out between notebooks and textbooks. But in a magnetic holder on the inner wall of the locker, a few pencils and a hairbrush sit, awaiting us.

"Let's do this quickly," I say, glancing around. Now that Rena's locker is open, this feels suddenly illicit, like we can get caught at any minute. How do we explain the open lock, the slime, the two of us in school so late at night? Gayil can talk her way out of anything, but I'm a terrible liar. "Where do you want to put the slime?"

"Between the bristles," Gayil says, opening the container of clear, yellow-tinted slime. "She'll probably realize right after she starts brushing, but she'll get a little bit of slime stuck in those curls beforehand. She's going to be so confused." She sounds gleeful. "A Fairview mystery. No one will ever figure us out."

Maybe it's just because I've never really had a best friend, but the idea of getting slime stuck in someone's hair makes me uneasy. But I don't question it. If Gayil wants a grand mystery, then Gayil will get it, and it'll all turn out perfectly in the end. That's just how Gayil works. And if this is a secret between me and Gayil . . . well, maybe we'll even be friends at the end of this.

I step back and watch Gayil drop the slime into the wide bristles of the brush. It's too firm, a little ball of goo instead of sliding between the bristles, and Gayil makes a face. "I need something to press it in," she says, and she opens my locker and pulls out a pencil. "Hey, Camp Kinor solidarity," she says cheerfully, grinning at the logo on the side of the pencil as though she'd forgotten that I'd been in camp with her this summer. She pushes the slime with the pencil, coating the entire tip of it and pressing the rest against the back of the brush. "There we go," she says, sounding very pleased with her handiwork. She twists the brush around to show me. "You can barely even see it."

"Cool," I say, though I am still uncertain about this. "What does slime do to—"

A door closes somewhere down the hallway and around the corner, and we jump. The pencil drops out of Gayil's hand into the depths of Rena's locker, and we stare at each other. "Run," Gayil whispers. "I'll lock it up again. Get out of here before they find you!"

There are loud footsteps, the clomping gait of the school custodian somewhere nearby, and I hesitate, ready to run. "Wait," I say, fighting my own instincts. "I'm not leaving you here. Quickly—"

We jam the lock back on and hurry to the stairs, a nervous giggle escaping my mouth like a tiny shriek. "Hello?" calls a booming voice, and Gayil yanks my hand and pulls me into the stairwell before we can be seen, both of us dashing down the stairs and then taking off down the hallway. Gayil glides on her Heelys, much faster than me, and I run after her, panting, with my heart pounding.

We make it out of the playground and across the street without being noticed, and we surge back to the safety of the development before we finally stop moving. Gayil catches my eye and then we're both laughing, overwhelmed with adrenaline and our own daring, and she says, "Shaindy, we *have* to get you on Rollerblades for next time."

"Next time," I agree, and it settles like a happy little *maybe* in my heart.

There's going to be a next time. Next time, again, it'll be Gayil and me.

CHAPTER 4

It's an unpleasant shock when Gayil rolls past me the next morning, cruising down the street of the development, and completely ignores me as though I don't exist. Rena and Devorah are with her, moving too quickly for me to catch up, and I wonder if Gayil just hadn't seen me.

But by the time I trudge into the school building, I'm sure that it's intentional. Gayil's gaze passes right through me when I'm at my locker next to Rena. I glance at her out of the corner of my eye to see if she's found the slime. I even say hi to her as we walk into our homeroom together, and she looks at me as though I'm a stranger and gives me a vague smile.

I bite my lip, my excitement from the day before fading away. Gayil and I aren't friends. Whatever has happened, it isn't going to change who I am in school. I'm the shadow, the girl no one notices, and I doodle in my notebook and listen moodily to Morah Neuman as she presents our Succos project.

"I'm sure some of you already have your Succah up," she says in her reedy, always wry voice. Morah Neuman is one of the older teachers in the school, tall and stern and engaging, and I can never quite tell when she's serious or speaking in a dead pan. This time, I'm confident enough to laugh about it. No one has a Succah up this early. By Succos, the identical patios behind every house in the development will have a little square hut up inside it, made from wood or plastic panels or canvas wrapped around metal poles, and we'll all eat outside in them and sing Succos songs together across the strip of backyards. But Succos isn't for another three weeks, and no one around here thinks about putting up their Succahs before Rosh Hashanah.

"All right," Morah Neuman concedes. "It *is* a little early to start on a Succos project. But your Succos vacation is going to start in two weeks, just before Yom Kippur, and this project is a little involved. We're going to put twenty minutes into it every morning before we daven, and we'll learn a bit about Rosh Hashanah and Yom Kippur while you work on it."

The projects this year are big foam boards wrapped in black velvet with elaborate designs in thin grey lines across them. We're each given ten bags with different colored sequins in them and another bag full of pins, and we're supposed to follow the lines, pushing pins in through the sequin holes to decorate the board. It looks hard, but it'll be beautiful when it's done, and I get to work right away, pushing thoughts of Gayil from my mind.

She's whispering to Rena near the front of the room, comparing their boards and showing hers to a few other girls, and Morah Neuman raises her white-blond eyebrows and says, "Gayil, I know that you'd make a phenomenal teacher someday, but this room already has one."

Gayil grins, apologetic and charming, and Morah Neuman shakes her head. "On that note, let's discuss the four steps of teshuva. What is teshuva?"

I stare at my board, calculating how many sequins I have of each color. There is a Hebrew phrase at the center of the board, *v'samachta b'chagecha*, and flowers adorn each of the swirling lines around it. If I use only the lighter colors, I can create a kind of iridescence in the flowers.

"Teshuva means *repentance*," soft-spoken Tzivia Krasner says from the seat behind me. I push my pins in, focused on my task and listening with half an ear. "Like when you stop doing something wrong."

"It's a bit more than that," Morah Neuman informs us. "Stopping might make things better from then on, but teshuva isn't just stopping but *erasing* what has been done. On Yom Kippur, we want to come out refreshed, like new people who've done a full teshuva. Step One is stopping. But there are four steps. Anyone remember from last year?"

Gayil's hand shoots up. "You have to feel bad about it," she says. "Charata, right?"

"And then you have to admit it," Ariella says. She sits in the back corner near the row of tall, wide windows, and her long fingers are nimble on her board, sticking pins through sequins like she'll be done in days instead of weeks. "And decide you won't do it again."

"Right. Four steps." Morah Neuman nods with satisfaction. "There is no teshuva without all four steps. It's about stripping away our pride and admitting that we were wrong; because without that, how can we ever undo it? How can we ever stop ourselves from doing it again? And there's another step too, when we're talking about wrongs committed toward someone else. Shaindy?"

I jump in my seat and stab myself with a pin by accident. I don't raise my hand if I can help it, and Morah Neuman is one of those teachers who will call on anyone she suspects might be inattentive. "Uh," I try. My mind is blank, as though I haven't been listening even though I *have* been, and Morah Neuman watches me with disapproval.

Tzivia nudges me. "Sorry," she mutters, and it takes me a second to realize that she's given me the answer.

"You have to apologize," I say, unsticking the pin from the side of my finger. "It's not just about erasing what you've done, but about erasing the hurt from the other person too." Everyone does that on the last day of school before Yom Kippur, the dance of *sorry-do-you-forgive-me?* that doesn't really mean anything and demands only one response. You can't say *no* and get in the way of someone else's teshuva. It's mean and spiteful to do that, and my class is anything but mean.

Morah Neuman looks very pleased. "Well done, girls. You really know your stuff." She moves through the aisles of desks, pausing at the back of the room. "There is an opinion that, if you sincerely ask someone for forgiveness three times, then you're in the clear. You've done your part. But what does 'sincere apology' mean? I want you to think about that over the next day, until we get back to this tomorrow." It's time to put our boards away, and there's a low murmur through the room as we tuck them into the metal shelves that are attached to the bottom of each chair.

I twist around to Tzivia. "Thanks," I whisper. Tzivia smiles at me. She's got her own friends and isn't interested in being mine, I guess, but we'd been together in the summer while her friends had gone to a day camp in Fairview. We'd been kind of like friends then, and we'd spent some time together.

"I hate when Morah Neuman calls on random girls," she whispers back. "It's so stressful. I always raise my hand first so she won't try me." She runs an olive-brown hand through her messy brown hair, casting a nervous eye at the front of the room. I turn back, catch Morah Neuman's disapproving look, and try to sit very straight.

Gayil gets up suddenly, grabbing one of the two bathroom passes at the front of the room and sauntering out, and Morah Neuman looks more bemused than disapproving of her. I wonder what she'd think of Gayil if she knew where we'd been last night. Knowing Gayil and how much everyone loves her, Morah Neuman would probably think it was charming.

I'm frustrated again. Hadn't I been there with Gayil last night? Doesn't that earn me *something*? I don't expect to be suddenly popular or even noticed, but Gayil could at least say *hi*. She could at least smile at me.

I get up, grab the second bathroom pass, and follow her down the hall. "Gayil," I call, earning a sharp look from a teacher passing by. The other classes are already davening, singing prayers in unison, and it filters into the hallways. "Gayil," I say again, this time lower.

She doesn't respond, just disappears into the bathroom, and I hurry after her. When I get inside, she's already in a stall, and I wait impatiently near the sinks, tapping a foot against the tile.

She emerges from a stall a minute later, and she washes her hands as though I'm not there. "*Gayil*," I say again, and I'm embarrassed at how my voice cracks, how pleading I sound.

Gayil looks up at last, catching my eyes in her fierce ones, and I fall silent. "We have to be careful in school," she says slowly, as if I'm very stupid. "Shaindy, if we suddenly start hanging out when all of these pranks start, don't you think people are going to get suspicious?"

Maybe I *am* very stupid. "Oh," I say, and it washes over me like a wave of relief. "That makes sense."

"No one will ever know that it's us," Gayil says, and her eyes glitter again, that mischief bright on her face. "We'll be the last ones they suspect." She puts her hand in mine and squeezes it. She's wearing her charm bracelet, the one that everyone else in the class had gotten last year as soon as Gayil had. Today, it has a hanging heart that bumps against my skin. She has a dozen different charms that she swaps out daily. I have a bracelet too, but my charm is a little *S*, and I wear the same one every day.

The heart is golden and smooth, and it's cool against the tip of my middle finger. "Our secret," Gayil breathes, and she slips away, leaving me behind in the bathroom.

I wait there for a few minutes, just to be safe, and when I return to the room, no one looks twice at me. Only I can see out the curl of Gayil's lips, the approving smile as she sings the prayers with everyone else, and I feel warm all over.

CHAPTER 5

I t happens after lunch.

I spend most of morning recess in a state of anticipation and dread. We get twenty-five minutes in the morning, spent in the school's second yard. The first, of course, is the playground for the younger kids where Gayil and I had sneaked into the school. The second has no playground, no bars to swing on or slides to climb. I miss them sometimes, because I'd had much more to do on them than I ever have in this empty yard.

Some kids play ball in the center of the blacktop, but most girls have retrieved their Rollerblades from their lockers and are circling the yard. The only girls on the ground are Sheva, writing in a notebook with Tammy doing splits beside her, and me. I sit against the chain-link fence on the side of the yard, eating my snack and glancing over at Gayil and Rena where they're rollerblading on their Heelys on the opposite side of the yard.

Still no sign of the slime. I'm relieved though a part of me is disappointed. I've spent the morning on edge, waiting for *something* to happen, and now it seems like my whole adventure with Gayil has been for nothing. Is she going to want to continue the pranks after this disappointing first attempt?

I'm distracted from my thoughts by a Rollerblade that nearly crashes into me, zipping to the side and stopping short. The Rollerblade is a dingy one, and it's attached to thick, grey knee socks and a plaid grey skirt, topped off by a light blue polo and Tzivia's worried face peering down at me. "Sorry!" she says, chagrined. "I nearly crashed into you. Are you okay?"

I smile up at her. Tzivia is sweet, even if we aren't really friends. "I'm fine. You stopped right in time."

"Oh, good." She looks relieved. "Hey, do you want to borrow my Rollerblades for a bit? We still have another ten minutes and I wanted to eat something."

I blink at her. "What?"

Tzivia shrugs, a self-conscious finger twirling through her mousy brown hair until some of it is pulled free from her ponytail. "You keep looking over at everyone rollerblading. I thought you might want a go-around with mine."

Of course. Because the only reason why I might not be rollerblading is because I don't have Rollerblades of my own. I chew on my lip and consider giving them a try. Maybe it's just my sister's Rollerblades that make it so hard to master. Or maybe I'll just embarrass myself even more. "Thanks," I say finally. "I'm just not really into rollerblading."

"Oh." Tzivia sits next to me, her Rollerblades clattering as she drops. "Well, let me know if you change your mind." She opens a bag of chips that had been clutched in her hand and offers one to me. I eat it in silence. Another girl comes to sit with Tzivia, chatting with her about a book they'd both read, and her attention is dragged from me.

Which is fine. I'm still watching Rena, waiting for nothing to happen.

And nothing does happen, right until we return from lunch.

One minute, we're all swarming back upstairs from the lunch-room with our bags, ducking into our lockers as we prepare for math class. The next, Rena is beside me, her brush out as she chats with Gayil, and I know that she's about to do what she always does after lunch. She sprays her hair absently with a spray bottle, wetting it, and then she pulls out her brush as I fiddle around in my locker.

"My father is making the *cutest* desserts for Rosh Hashanah with me," she says, running the brush through her damp hair.

Gayil laughs. "Your father does the baking?"

"My mother doesn't have the patience," Rena says, making a face. "She's an awesome cook, but whenever she has to follow a recipe, she just gives up. She says that it's a math-brain thing, and she's too creative for that." I know that Rena's mother is an *artist*. In the after-noons, she gives art classes in her house on the other side of our development, her tichel never quite covering up the stray wild curls that escape the front of it.

Rena's curls are better tamed, and I dart a glance at her and discover with horror that the slime is being ground into her hair by the brush as she moves it through the curls. Gayil says, "So what are the desserts? Something with apples, I bet."

"Basically, you wrap cut apples in dough to make them into roses," Rena says. She doesn't seem to notice the gleam of slime in her hair, and Gayil gives nothing away. "You're going to *love* them when I bring them over. Should I come for the first-day meal or the second night?"

"I was thinking about the first day," Gayil says easily. The brush has only the faintest glistening moisture on it now, the rest of the slime already transferred to Rena's hair. "That way we can spend the day together and then you'll sleep over."

Devorah joins them, her freckled nose wrinkling as she looks down at them. Devorah looks down at most people, not by personality—she's friends with everyone and is genuinely nice—but because she's already taller than some of our teachers. "Rena, your hair's all gooey," she says.

Rena doesn't look alarmed. "It's probably the new mousse I put in it," she says, shrugging. "Gayil and I picked it out on Sunday at the shopping center. It's supposed to reactivate every time I get my hair wet and I just massage it back in." She runs her fingers through her hair, coating it all with slime, and I watch her and feel very sick.

But she doesn't realize that anything is wrong. She doesn't know what we've done, not at first. Instead, we are busy in math class, reviewing fractions from last year, and Mrs. Gelman eyes Rena once and looks puzzled but says nothing. Even Gayil is beginning to look impatient, waiting for her prank to be figured out, but Rena doesn't seem to notice. I watch her from my seat, off to the far side of the math class, and I feel sicker and sicker as the day continues.

But there is nothing. We read a short story in ELA, and then we calculate latitude and longitude in social studies. It isn't until science class when Mrs. Beim, our last teacher of the day, calls Rena over and whispers to her in a low voice.

"No," Rena says, shaking her head. "It's this new product—it's kind of itchy, but it's not—"

"Rena," Mrs. Beim says gently, "I think you might have slime in your hair."

Rena looks horrified. "*What?*" she says, and she touches her hair again, runs a hand through it, and I watch as the dawning horror starts to build on her face. "What?" she says again, and now she looks as though she might cry.

Mrs. Beim says, "I'll write the office a note so you can call home and sign out early. Try conditioner—or mayonnaise, if the conditioner doesn't work," she suggests.

Rena's voice is shrill. "*I am not putting mayonnaise in my hair!*" she shouts, and Mrs. Beim looks taken aback. "Who put slime in my hair?" she demands, whirling around. "It wasn't like this this morning. I *felt* it. It happened at lunch, or—"

We are all transfixed by Rena's distress, and I shudder beneath it, suddenly sure that everyone knows exactly who'd done it. The guilt must be written all over my face, and I shrink back, my hands shaking around my pencil. But Rena's eyes move over me like she doesn't know I exist, and I try to breathe, my heart still beating so quickly that I'm positive that everyone around me can hear it.

It's Gayil who speaks. She isn't shaking. Her eyes are steady, a hint of concern in them, and her light brown face looks shadowed and sincere. I should have guessed that she's a great actor because she's so good at everything else, but it comes as a surprise that she'd dare to do what she does next, which is to say, "Rena, was there any slime in your locker?"

Rena lets out a little noise, a squeak of horror, and she shakes her head and dashes out of the classroom. Mrs. Beim sighs. "It's a little like gum in your hair," she says to the rest of us. "Slime can damage and dry out your hair though. It's one of the reasons why we banned slime in school. Too many parents complaining about the slime getting everywhere—on clothes, on notes, and in hair. It's a pain in the neck."

We can all hear the cry of outrage in the hall, and then the sound of a girl running down it, her footfalls hard as they pound against the floor. I shift in my seat, the guilt like a flash of discomfort through me, and I hope that it's going to be okay. I don't like Rena very much—I don't *dislike* her either, it wouldn't be nice to dislike a girl just for being smart and popular and friends with a girl like Gayil—but she doesn't deserve this. We'd just meant for it to be a little practical joke, nothing so serious. Just a distraction from school. Gayil had picked Rena *because* she's her friend, and had been so sure that it would be no big deal. She must be horrified now.

But when I peer over at Gayil, sitting in the center of the room with an empty desk beside her, she doesn't look regretful or horrified. Instead, a smile is playing at the edges of her lips, and she leans over to whisper something to Devorah. Devorah wiggles her eyebrows at Gayil, Rena's horror forgotten, and they both return to their notes as Mrs. Beim begins again.

Gayil's lack of concern reassures me. I'm blowing this out of proportion, and I'm building it into something that it isn't. Rena is fine, just a little shocked, and everyone knows that she's vain about her hair. She'll take a shower and wash out the slime, and everyone will wonder about it tomorrow. It'll just be a mystery that will linger, and Rena is only being dramatic.

I walk home with this certainty, my steps light as I wonder what Gayil might have planned for tonight. Will we go back to the school? Obviously, we'll have to be more careful this time to do something harmless. We hadn't *meant* to agitate Rena so much. Maybe it'll be something like the tricks we do for Purim, spiders in someone's locker or a secret walkie-talkie in the ceiling that we can use to confuse the class.

I do my homework quickly, shuffle through math and Chumash at the dining room table so that Bayla can work upstairs. "I'm going out to rollerblade after this," I tell Ema when she comments on how soon I'm done. "I want to get better."

I move unsteadily on the patio, but now there is new determination to it. I have to get better to keep up with Gayil. I need to earn those Heelys, just like Gayil, because who knows how long we'll be doing this together? And if we ever do anything else . . . if this awakens a friendship with someone like Gayil . . . well, I'll want to have Heelys for that too.

I am dreaming of it, rollerblading down the street to school with Gayil and Rena and Devorah, when I see Gayil step out of her house to her own patio. "I'm going to Devorah's!" she calls out, and someone responds from inside.

And then she steps down her patio and crosses the grass to mine, grinning when she sees my Rollerblades. "You got them!" she says.

"I'm not very good," I admit, flushing under her attention.

Gayil waves that away. "You just need practice. Come on," she says, and she tugs my hand, pulling me to her in a smooth movement. "I have the *perfect* place for that."

She takes my hand again once I've clomped over the grass and am wobbling in the street, and we roll down the smooth pavement together.

CHAPTER **6**

We're out a little earlier tonight, though it's already dark out. The boys at the high school across from our school are still there in full force, buses loading up and carpools pulling down the street. "They'll see us," I point out.

Gayil nods. "That's what I like about you, Shaindy," she says, grinning. "You're good at this sneaky stuff. What do you think we should do?"

I pause, considering. Last time, Gayil had been the one leading, and I'd just followed her through her plans. I hadn't expected to make any of the decisions this time. *I'm good at this sneaky stuff.* Gayil says it with such authority that I believe her. "We're just rollerblad-ing," I say. "Why wouldn't we go up and down the school block? It has the best sidewalks."

They're wide sidewalks, smooth and flat, and Gayil pulls me along a little as I hobble across the street. "You're doing it wrong," she says critically. "Push with one foot. Good. Now—wait!" I've already slipped, my foot tilting inward, and Gayil seizes my hand and holds me upright. "You have to put your other foot down *after* you push," she says, and she turns around, holding on to my hands as she faces me. "Try it again."

"I'm just not good at this stuff," I say, biting my lip. "I don't think I can rollerblade."

"Of course you can." Gayil scoffs. "I literally picked this up in an hour on the day after camp. It's not hard at all."

"Not for you," I point out. "You're good at . . . sporty kinds of things. I've seen you ice skating on school trips. I could trip over my own feet if I'm not careful." I stare glumly at my Rollerblades, then at Gayil, before I try again. The differences between us have never felt so pronounced. Gayil is tall and willowy, unmistakably pretty. Her skin is a shade of light brown that only a few girls in our class share, and the black hair behind her headband is long and straight with a little bit of a natural wave to it. She's the kind of girl who winds up on the cover of the weekly school newsletter, who could make anything look effortless.

I'm short. *Jewish average*, my doctor assures me, but on the shorter side of average, and I never quite lost the pudge that had made me cute and sweet looking when I'd been a toddler. My hair is a boring brown, and it curls in no discernible pattern and frizzes up even in a ponytail. Next to Gayil, I'm awkward even without saying a word. Of *course* I can't rollerblade. I can barely run without falling down.

But Gayil just laughs, guiding me forward along the sidewalk. "Please," she says. "You're good on your feet and you're strong. I always see you taking out the garbage on the side of the house. You just swing it *like*—" She makes a motion with her hands, a mock toss of a garbage bag into the cans, and I blink at her and don't know if I should be flattered or offended. "I bet you'll be fast once you get the hang of it. And you've been doing just fine since I let go, so I think you've got it—" I realize suddenly that Gayil isn't holding on to me, and I yelp, slipping against the hard black gate around the playground as Gayil laughs at me.

"Come on," she says, skating off. "I'll race you."

"*Wait!*" But the movements are a little easier now, and I'm not just dragging my feet as much as gliding, some of the time. Gayil still beats me to the corner, but I sort of rollerblade down most of it, and Gayil looks very pleased when she catches me before I slam into a traffic light pole.

"Easy," she says, sliding down the next sidewalk.

"Easy," I agree, dazed at what I'd just picked up. "My parents promised me Heelys if I figured out rollerblading," I blurt out next, and then regret it. Gayil doesn't care about what gifts I might be getting soon.

But Gayil grins. "That's great," she says. "Are the Rollerblades your sister's?"

I nod. "She never really got into it, so they've just been sitting in her closet. She gets everything first," I say, and I try not to sound too resentful.

Gayil laughs. "I've never gotten anything first," she agrees. "Two older sisters and three younger ones mean that we just pass them down as we grow out of them. It must be nice to just have the one sister. Different," she says, the understatement of the year. "But nice."

"I have two older brothers, but they're away in yeshiva in Miami," I say. "Bayla isn't *nice*. She treats me like I'm five and spends most of the time trying to get rid of me."

Gayil snorts. "None of my sisters would try. Too many to count. We're all outnumbered by the rest of us." She tilts her head. "It took four years in Bais Yaakov before teachers stopped accidentally calling me Bracha."

"Really?" I look at Gayil, mentally comparing her to her older sister. Bracha is kind enough—she used to walk me to school when I was little, trailing behind her sisters—but she doesn't have the presence that Gayil does.

Gayil tosses her hair. "I learned how to make myself memorable," she says, and she winks at me and takes off on her Heelys again. I follow her, trying to imagine a Gayil who *doesn't* stand out, who isn't the first name that teachers remember in our class. There's no way. Her fourth year in Bais Yaakov would have been second grade, and I still remember the envy I'd felt around her and her friends even then.

I rollerblade after her, panting as I try to keep up, and I circle the next block. At that point I nearly lose sight of Gayil, turning the next corner. But I'm getting faster. Gayil's Heelys aren't as fast as Rollerblades, and I'm beginning to find my balance in them, whipping down the next block and slamming into Gayil before I can figure out how to stop.

We both go down, laughing helplessly. "I'm sorry!" I say, but Gayil is still laughing, face tilted up to the emerging stars and her hands waving in careless response.

"You really just shot right into me," she says, shaking her head. "I can't *believe* it. Look at you—" And I notice the way that she's staring at me, like I've actually done something incredible. Like I *matter*, and a shiver edges its way down my spine as I stare at her.

Her gaze flickers into something uncomfortable, and I scramble to my feet, wincing at my heavy Rollerblades as they bang against her. "Sorry," I say again. "Sorry."

"Don't worry about it." Her voice is airy again, though there's something I can't read in her eyes. "Come on. I bet the boys are gone by now."

We glide together around the next block that wraps around the school, and I note with satisfaction that the high school is empty now. We can sneak into Fairview Bais Yaakov just like we did last night, and it's easier now, less nerve-racking. I'm getting used to this.

I have to pull off my Rollerblades to go up the steps to our classroom, and it makes this all feel even more illicit. My socks are silent next to Gayil's loud Heelys soles, and I lead the way, opening the classroom door and peering inside. "What are we doing today?" I ask, and I remember Rena's despair earlier. "How's . . . did Rena get the slime out?"

Gayil shrugs. "She'll be fine," she says airily. "It's just Rena. She's *so* dramatic." I've never heard anyone talk about Rena like that, and I stare at her, wide-eyed. It's not what I'd expect from perfect Gayil, who is known for being all the things that embody our community: giving and thoughtful and polite and *never* prone to gossip about her friends.

In a nasty little part of me, it feels good to hear it.

I swallow. "We're not pulling a prank on Devorah today, are we?" That would place the blame solidly on Gayil, and I'm suddenly worried for her. This might seem harmless, but if Gayil gets in trouble for it—

Gayil shakes her head. "No," she says. "This time, we're going to pull the prank on the whole class. Something that they can't ignore." She opens a locker, seemingly at random, and she amends, "Well, anyone without a lock on their locker."

I look around, wary. Only a few girls lock their lockers, and most of them forget to keep them sealed in the rush to leave during dismissal. Three are locked, and two more have the locks hanging open.

Everyone else is *ours*. I can feel the exhilaration going, the certainty that this is going to be fun. "What are we going to do?"

"A little switcheroo," Gayil says in a singsong voice. "Easy. *Baffling*. And the class will never recover from the Fairview Bandits." She nudges against me, her eyes glittering with excitement, and I can feel her enthusiasm pass over me and catch, abruptly, in my heart, like a wind that you can feel to your core.

CHAPTER 7

It's definitely a prank that no one can ignore. I open my locker the next morning and pull out my notebook, only to discover that it's been replaced with someone else's notebook. "Huh," I say aloud, just in case someone's listening.

No one is, of course. I could probably get up in the middle of class, take off my uniform and reveal a shiny leotard under it, and then sing at the top of my lungs, and no one would notice. But around me, other girls are just as confused. "Temima, is this yours?" says Devorah, stooping down to stare at her locker in bewilderment. "You must have mixed up our lockers yesterday."

Temima shakes her head, sniffling back her perpetually runny nose in the process. "No way. I don't have your notebook." She squints at hers. "This kind of looks like Chana Leah's handwriting."

"That's mine," Chana Leah agrees. She holds up a notebook. "Anyone missing this?"

There's chaos by the time Morah Neuman makes it to our class-room, girls holding up notebooks and trying to find the right ones. I spot Gayil in one corner, raising a colorful notebook with a picture of someone's chubby-cheeked nephew taped to the back.

"Anyone? Still looking for mine," she says, and she looks bemused, not an ounce of guilt on her face.

"Mine," someone says, taking the notebook from my hand. "Have you seen yours?" It's Tzivia who is looking at me, her blue eyes concerned, and I muster up all the acting skills that I'd gained from my two-line performance in the camp play.

"Not yet. This is so *weird*." I wander through the crowd, peering around for someone who hasn't paired up their notebook yet. Morah Neuman is shouting something over the crowd of girls, but no one can hear her. Gayil has reclaimed her notebook. I'm looking for Tammy, whom I'm pretty sure I'd given mine to.

I find her with Sheva, her best friend. Tammy is the class gymnast, and Sheva is the best creative writer in the class. They'd been in camp with us but hadn't spent much time with everyone else, always bent over notebooks and scribbling frantically like it had still been school. They used to pass one back and forth, writing grand stories together, and I see them doing the same at recess sometimes too.

"Is that mine?" I say, pointing at Tammy's notebook, and she passes it absently to me.

Sheva looks pale under her shock of orange curls, her eyes red rimmed, and Tammy says, "We'll find it. Everyone just has someone else's—it's not a big deal—"

"I don't see it *anywhere*," Sheva says, and she takes a shuddering breath. "Look. My school notebook is *here*—" She holds up a second notebook, and I step back when she glares suddenly at me. "What do you want?"

"Nothing," I say quickly. "I was just—getting my notebook—"
I stumble back away from them, uncertain what I'd just witnessed,
and I turn to see how everyone else is doing. *The Fairview Bandits strike
again*, I think, a little overwhelmed at my own audacity.

We're all distracted from the chaos when a loud, shrill whistle
sounds from somewhere near the entrance to the classroom. "Inside!"
Morah Neuman calls, her fingers still at her lips. "To your desks!
We will work this out *inside*."

There is a flurry of activity. Tzivia finds me again in the chaos,
and I hold up my notebook to her concerned gaze. Sheva is the last
to enter, clutching her school notebook with an expression of devastation on her face. Gayil orders people to sit, at ease as Morah
Neuman's lieutenant. Somehow, Morah Neuman gets us all seated,
and she collects notebooks from the last five or six girls who haven't
found their match yet. "Anyone's?" she says, holding one up.

"I am *so* glad I lock my locker," says a girl near the front of the
room with close-cropped hair. I don't recognize her for a moment,
and then I gape, realizing exactly who she is. *Rena*. Rena's hair is all
but gone, cut nearly to her head, and she looks strange with that
narrow neck and face and no hair to frame it. She scowls suddenly.
"Not that it helped with whoever *slimed my brush*."

Gayil snorts. "Rena, are you sure that wasn't *you*? You've been
sneaking slime into school for two years." Her face is guileless,
politely skeptical of Rena's accusation, and I admire Gayil's acting
ability again.

Rena rolls her eyes. "*Please.* I'm eleven, not nine. I'm over it."
But there is a tic in her jaw when she speaks, a frustration that she
doesn't name. I pull my project out from the basket under my chair

and work on getting sequins onto pins. I'm sure that my face is red, but no one seems to notice.

None of the missing notebooks are Sheva's though, and I see her put her head down as Morah Neuman walks out, burying it in her arms. We busy ourselves with our projects, but there's a strange undercurrent in the room, a sudden distrust as classmates stare at each other. "Who did it?" Sari whispers to Meira next to me, her voice too loud in the quiet. "Why would someone do this?"

"At least everyone got their notes back," Devorah says, and Rena and Gayil nod in perfect unison. "I'd have been *mad* if mine were gone. I color-code everything." She shows her notebook to Rena, who makes admiring noises. "Maybe this is some kind of social experiment."

Gayil snorts. "*You're* a social experiment," she says, nudging Devorah, and the mood in the room seems to calm with the three of them, more smiles and less unease.

That lasts until Morah Neuman returns with the principal. Mrs. Teichman is grim faced, and she glances around the room with a sweeping, stern gaze. She's the kind of principal everyone's afraid of, even though she isn't *mean*, just strict. At our junior high orientation, she talked about *consequences* so forcefully that Temima cried.

"I was shocked to hear that the chaos this morning was from this class," she says without preamble, and we all look up, our eyes wide and anxious. "*This class* in particular, I have always heard, embodies what a Bais Yaakov girl should be. The girls here are respectful of their teachers, of their surroundings, and of each other. This is a class known for your good middos!"

A few girls look down, shamefaced, even though they hadn't done a thing. I can't seem to stop my eyes from racing at the same pace as my heartbeat, glancing from girl to girl to Morah Neuman to Mrs. Teichman. "Good middos doesn't just mean *well-behaved*," Mrs. Teichman clarifies. "It means that Bais Yaakov girls carry themselves differently. You are all regal princesses," she says, and this is a speech we've heard before. "Modest, thoughtful, and certainly not prone to *practical jokes*. I'm very disappointed in you," she says, and her gaze bores into each of us, one by one. "This isn't what I expected of you."

I feel very much like the worst person ever, right up until I sneak a glance at Gayil and see her doodling, looking bored. There is no guilt in her eyes, and I take a breath and try not to take any of this seriously. Mrs. Teichman is blowing a tiny prank out of proportion. She's the *principal*. It's her job to ban fun.

Mrs. Teichman continues, talking about how we need to be more aware of everyone else's feelings when Yom Kippur is so close, and I tune her out and let my eyes glaze over. By the end, the class is silent, and Morah Neuman looks satisfied. "I don't want to see anything like this again," she says. "Now, let's get back to the four steps of teshuva."

But she isn't so fortunate. Gayil and I sneak in again the next night, this time with a little bee trap that her family hangs on the patio. "They're not *wasps*," Gayil says when I look warily at it. "There are, like, three of them in here. I bet we can slip them into Morah Neuman's closet and see how everyone *freaks* at them. The windows will be open," she reminds me, and she puts the trap into the closet, opening it with the doors still half closed around her arm. "It's harmless."

And she's right, as Gayil always is. The bees escape halfway through Hebrew the next morning when Morah Neuman opens her closet, and the entire class turns upside down, shrieking at the top of our lungs until even Morah Neuman can't calm us down. Sari hides under her desk, sobbing in that too-loud voice of hers, "I'm allergic! I'm going to *die!*" and Morah Neuman finally gives up on quieting the classroom and sends us all into the hall.

The bees are gone a minute later, out the window to sail off and bother some other class. Sari is still out in the hallway and refuses to go back inside for the rest of the class, but everyone else thinks of it as a funny incident, nothing more. We'd done it, another prank completed, and I don't think anything of it until the end of the day.

Mrs. Teichman comes in, and she says, "*No more,*" in that resounding, terrifying voice. "If I see one more prank from this class, I *will* find out who's behind it, and we *will* look at detentions, or even suspensions. Zero tolerance," she says, and my skin crawls.

But when I glance over at Gayil, she doesn't look bored or cowed by Mrs. Teichman's threats. Instead, she looks defiant, her lip curled and her eyes hard. I straighten my back and shove away my fears.

CHAPTER 8

The next day is Friday, and Gayil and I don't do anything tonight. We don't have school tomorrow because we're all busy getting ready for Rosh Hashanah, which is tomorrow night. It's two days of holiday, which means four big family meals and long hours of prayers in the mornings, and I'm a little less excited than I usually am. For one thing, it falls on Saturday and Sunday this year, so I'm barely missing any school for it. For another, it might be *days* before I get to spend time with Gayil again.

Being around Gayil transforms me, I decide, looking at myself in the mirror. I'm still the same old Shaindy, but there is something different about me now. I carry myself a little taller, and I'm not slumping at the shoulders. I can rollerblade now, and I've made the most popular girl in school laugh a few times. I'm still Shaindy, but Shaindy might be someone special, after all.

Even Ema looks at me in surprise when I come downstairs that afternoon and says, "Shaindy, you're looking cheerful." She's cooking, and she has her hair clipped up into a blue headscarf that is loose at the bottom. Her round face is dotted with sauce, her clothes dusted with flour, and she smells vaguely of potato kugel. "Excited for Rosh Hashanah?"

"Yeah," I say, the easier answer. I wonder absently if Gayil will be around at all, or if Rena and Devorah will monopolize her. Last year, when I'd discovered that Gayil would be going to camp without Devorah, I'd been sure that it would be my moment, but Rena had signed up and Gayil had been out of reach again. Gayil's friends are *tight*, and I don't have a chance of slipping in.

Unless Gayil wants me there. If I go upstairs after the meal tonight and see Gayil in the window, this whole holiday off from pranking the class will be worth it.

"I could use a hand with setting the table for tonight," Ema says, and I obediently set the table, cut up onions, and then sauté vegetables for the chicken soup. Ema is in and out, making phone calls to her siblings and her parents before Rosh Hashanah to wish them a happy New Year, and I glance out the window of the kitchen and spot Gayil and one of her sisters in their kitchen, doing the same thing as me.

Gayil spots me and shoots me a smile, and I feel as though I'm a dozen feet tall. Behind me, Ema says, "Oh, it's good to see you getting along with Avigayil Itzhaki. How has school been this year?"

"Better than usual," I say truthfully, and then, in a less truthful explanation, "We're doing this really cool project in school for Succos."

Ema raises her eyebrows at me as though she knows that I'm leaving something out. "Have you gotten closer to any of the girls from camp?" she says gently. "Avigayil or . . . Sari Klein was there, wasn't she? And Tammy Seidenbaum?"

I can't mention Gayil, though I crave telling *someone* about her. Ema would never approve of what we've been doing, even if it did make me a new friend. "Tzivia Krasner and I hang out a little in school," I say. "It's still really early in the year, but I think it's going to be a good one."

"Good." Ema smiles at me, her round cheeks dimpling with the movement. "You're such a sensitive, creative girl, and I'm glad that you have a sweet class. I just wish that they'd be a little more open to including you." She rests a hand on my shoulder, and I squirm, feeling at once more pathetic than I have until now. I don't like to think of myself as an outcast, because I'm *not*. No one leaves me out intentionally. It's just that no one thinks of me first, or second, or sometimes even third. I'm invisible, not hated.

I'm relieved when Ema says, "Oh, no. Our new fruit is rotten." I peer over her shoulder into the fridge. The new fruit is a special addition for the New Year, something unusual that we haven't had in a full year. This one is a strange-looking brown fruit, shaped like a kidney and kind of fuzzy, and there is something black and putrid-looking at the center of it.

"I can pick up another one," I offer. I don't usually run errands—that's Bayla's job, because the shopping center where Shop It Glatt is located is across a major road—but I am feeling independent today, like I can do anything my older sister can.

Ema eyes me speculatively. "You *are* in sixth grade now," she says thoughtfully. "It might be time to let you go shopping for me." She motions to her bag, sitting on a dining room chair. "Take a twenty," she says. "Return it, get two new fruits and something small for yourself."

"Okay!" I grab the money and the fruit and maneuver them from hand to hand as I slide my feet into the Rollerblades and close the clasps. I ease down the stairs from the porch and glide into the street.

Ema calls after me, "And don't forget to look both ways or you will *die!*" which is her constant refrain whenever I go anywhere, and I lift a hand in concession and head out of the development.

Past the school, the streets start to change, still spaced with houses but these are less identical. Some have huge front yards, little boys with yarmulkes playing soccer and baseball on their lawns, but others are small and shabby, sporting cars in the driveways with battered bumpers and plastic taped across the back window. The smell of challah and chicken soup is everywhere, drifting through the streets like Rosh Hashanah has already begun.

Slowly, stores begin to emerge from the housing like the first blooms after winter: a narrow shop emblazoned with the words *SOCKS4U*; a house with the name of a charity organization over the door; and then a street of stores and parking lots, loud and busy and bursting with people. The next street is the big one, six lanes of traffic across it, and I brake my Rollerblades at the red light and wait as cars zip by me fast enough that I am unbalanced.

"Careful," says a voice next to me as I seize the traffic light pole. It's Tzivia, a bag slung over her elbow. She glances down at my feet. "Hey! I guess you did pick up rollerblading after all."

I bob my head. "Are you headed to Shop It Glatt too?" I ask curiously. There's a whole shopping center there, but the morning before Rosh Hashanah seems a poor time to go shopping for anything but food or clothes.

Tzivia nods. "Our new fruit is rotten," she says, holding up the bag and making a face.

"Ours too. We must have gotten the same thing." I laugh. "For all we know, that thing is supposed to look like it's rotten. But my mother didn't want to serve it at the table."

The light turns red and a wave of pedestrians cross the street in both directions. Tzivia has Rollerblades on too, hers a little shabbier than even mine. We glide together through the parking lot, keeping time with each other, and she says, "I always feel so rude when I'm rollerblading in the grocery store. But at this point, it feels like every kid over a certain age is doing it." She looks rueful. "They'll probably ban them in the store sometime soon."

"You rollerbladed in camp too," I remember suddenly. Tzivia had worn them before Heelys had been *in*, gliding through the tennis court with Sheva as Tammy had done cartwheels around them.

Tzivia nods. "Bet you didn't know I'm a trendsetter," she says, her voice teasing. "Before that, I always figured I was just the quiet, nerdy type."

"Quiet, *smart* type," I correct her. "You're, like, the top student in the class. Except maybe Gayil and Rena," I say thoughtfully, because I know how effortless their work is. I see them studying with Devorah sometimes, stretched out on the trampoline and ignoring their notebooks, and they still ace every test. Devorah, I think, struggles in school more. We're on the same reading track in school, just barely above grade level.

Tzivia rolls her eyes. "Barely," she says. "Everyone in our class is an overachiever. You know Rivky Klein from camp? She was in the other bunk." I do vaguely remember her, a girl from the next development over who is in a different class in our grade. "Anyway, she told me that her class had an average of eighty-six on their first Yedios Klaliyos test this year."

"Really?" Our class had managed an average of ninety-eight, though I'd only gotten an eighty-three. "That's just our class," I say, shrugging. "You know our reputation. It makes it even more impressive that you're on top of it."

We've reached the return counter, and we wait in line, our legs bent inward to keep from rolling forward. Tzivia says, "I guess. It gets very intense sometimes," she admits, and a little bit of weariness creeps into her voice. "Especially this year. Did you see the test schedule up near the door of the classroom? A bunch of teachers have already scheduled their first tests for the week after Succos. Sixth grade is *hard*."

I had noticed them, though I'd filed them away as problems for Future Shaindy. The first few weeks of school, before Rosh Hashanah and before Yom Kippur, never quite feel like school as much as an early taste of what's to come. I'm not ready to be in sixth grade yet, but now I have more of an idea of what I'll be dealing with soon.

We return our fruits. The man behind the counter barely glances at them, just puts a credit on the receipt and tells us to go pick out something else. "Careful on those Rollerblades," he says, rubbing the side of his scraggly beard. "I like those new rolling sneakers that I've been seeing on all the girls lately. What are they called?"

"Heelys," we say together, and he nods in satisfaction.

"Much less bulky," he says. "Go ahead, get your fruit. I'm sure you have plenty more to do for Rosh Hashanah." He passes us each a little honey candy, and we take them politely. I can't stand honey candy, but I don't tell him that. I only offer mine to Tzivia when we go down the next aisle.

She wrinkles her nose. "My mother's a teacher, and she brought home three separate gifts from students with honey candy. Does *anyone* like them?"

"My father drops them into tea and lets them dissolve," I offer. "But that's about it. And I think he only does it because they keep sticking them into our grocery bags." We're making our way through the vegetable aisle, moving slowly between harried shoppers seizing last-minute parsnips and carrots for soup.

Finally, we make it to the new fruits, all of them displayed in open boxes beneath a big banner reading, *NEW FRUITS* in Hebrew. "Oh, these are *weird*," Tzivia says, holding up a red fruit with what looks like yellow-green hair coming out of it. "Makes you want to just buy the starfruit."

The starfruit is a classic, green and oval with a bland taste and pretty, star-shaped pieces when you slice it. "Nah," I say. I've spotted something much more interesting. It looks like a dragon's egg, red with green skin rising from it like flames. "I'm getting one of these. And this one." There's a pinkish fruit that is sold in a bunch, each of them with rugged skin that reminds me of raspberries. "If the cool fruit is bad, we'll always have these."

"Not this?" Tzivia says teasingly, picking up the brown fruit we'd returned. "Looks . . . nice and fuzzy."

"Looks like an animal is about to pop out of it," I correct her, laughing. "A little napping place for maggots—"

Tzivia mimes vomiting. "You say the grossest things," she says, sighing in mock admiration. "I bet you were one of these fruits in a past life."

"I bet you were one of these," I say, plucking a fruit labeled *Horned Melon* from a box. "Subtle but *vicious*."

Tzivia pulls a face at me. "You'll never know." I'm giggling help-lessly, and on a less busy day, I might have attracted enough atten-tion to be considered immodest. It feels *nice* to be out here with someone who is kind of like a friend, moving through a store with someone else instead of being the odd girl, alone. I've always been lonely, but it's a surprise how much stronger that sense of loneliness gets when I have the chance to be with company.

And then, because I have a sense like no other for the friend of my dreams, I look to the right and spot Gayil. She's with Rena, pushing along a double stroller with two little siblings in it, and she pauses at a spot with free samples and kneels down in front of them to offer one to each. The little ones grab them, and Gayil says, her clear voice drifting toward us, "Make a bracha."

The little ones—Shlomit and Eitan, I remember vaguely—recite blessings from memory, and a few women stop to say amen when they're done. "Such sweet children," an older lady says, and Gayil smiles back, charming and modest.

"What a great big sister you have," says another, and Gayil turns to smile at her too, and catches sight of Tzivia and me.

I stand a little straighter, relieved that I'm not alone when Gayil sees me. *I do have friends*, I try to exude, and then I grin at Gayil and start to move toward her. "Come on, Tzivia," I say, tugging Tzivia along, but Tzivia hangs back. "What?"

Gayil looks swiftly away, whispering something to Rena, and Rena laughs and plucks something off the shelf and into her basket. I redden, remembering our agreement to keep our partnership secret, and I turn back to Tzivia. "I thought we could say hi to Rena and Gayil," I mumble.

"Oh." Tzivia sounds less than enthused about that.

It's over and done with, but I can't help but defend Gayil from Tzivia's disinterest. "Gayil's really nice," I say. "I know that they're really popular, but it's just because they're good girls. Everyone looks up to them."

Tzivia shrugs, her diminutive frame shifting with the movement. "I guess. I just . . . you know that time in camp? That game of hide-and-seek we played, remember?"

I nod. It had been during the last week of camp, when we'd officially had sports for the last activity of the day but the sports counselor had never showed up. I'd suggested we would play a game of hide-and-seek instead, up near the sports fields, and Gayil had agreed, to my surprise. It had been the first time all summer when I'd actually felt like a part of the group. "It was fun, wasn't it?"

But Tzivia looks troubled. "Yeah," she says. "But remember how Gayil decided to hide out where no one could find her? And she wouldn't come out when we called, even when it was dinnertime. I spent so much time stressing about her, and then she just showed up in the morning like she hadn't made us all worry. It felt . . . well, kind of manipulative. To disappear just to see what we'd do." She shrugs. "At the very least, it was selfish."

"I thought it was funny," I say, defensive. I'd told everyone that it was fine that she was still hiding, had convinced them to leave it alone. It had been a strange but not unwelcome feeling, being heard by everyone. "It's Gayil. She's a free spirit."

"My mother says that's just code for *does whatever she wants*," Tzivia says, and she must see something unpleasant on my face, because she lifts and drops her narrow shoulders again and says, "Anyway, are you doing anything on Rosh Hashanah? The first afternoon is pretty long after lunch."

It sounds almost like an overture, and I hesitate, torn. On one hand, I *never* get invited out. Sometimes, over the years, I would invite a girl over for Shabbos at my mother's behest. They would come with awkward smiles and conversation, and Ema would direct our play, encouraging us toward different games and toys until it all finally petered out. It is never natural, and it feels natural right now.

On the other hand, Tzivia has called Gayil *manipulative* and *selfish*. Is this the kind of friend that I want? Someone who doesn't like the closest thing I have to a friend? Beggars can't be choosers, but I can't help but feel that Gayil would be betrayed if she'd heard the things that Tzivia had said about her. And I don't want to betray *Gayil*, who is on a completely different tier than Tzivia and me.

I shrug. "It might be pretty busy. Davening ends late by us."

Tzivia falls silent, and she lingers in the store when I check out. I don't wave goodbye to her, and I spot Gayil on the checkout line next to mine, chatting with the cashier and popping a honey candy into her mouth. "I love these," she says.

I pull mine out of the shopping bag, unwrap it, and stick it into my mouth. It's too sweet, but it's not as bad as I remember.

CHAPTER 9

Rosh Hashanah is brought in by candles, lit by my mother in an elaborate silver candelabra, and by the sound of prayers drifting from the shuls through the streets of the development. I sit on the porch and listen to singing, close my eyes, and wonder about this New Year. My resolution for this year is to make real friends, to be noticed and liked by them, just like it is every Rosh Hashanah. This year, it feels attainable.

Gayil is on her porch too, bouncing another sister on her lap as she tries to pray the evening prayers. She waves at me, that familiar grin on her face, and when she calls, "Shana tova!" to me, I feel as though my resolution is already coming true.

I wander back inside after a few minutes to set the table. My brothers aren't here for Rosh Hashanah, still studying in Miami, so it's just Ema and Abba and Bayla and me. Our downstairs neighbors are coming tonight too, and I set up the folded high chair in the corner of the room for the baby.

Bayla is on our brown fabric couch, reading a magazine as she absentmindedly curls her short brown hair around a stubby finger, and I sit opposite her and flip through one of the local newspapers. I'm scanning the ads, bored, when Bayla looks up abruptly for what must be the first time in weeks and says, sounding startled, "That dress isn't hideous."

"Thanks," I say, making a face at her. "It was yours first."

"Yeah, I know. I hated it on me. But it looks good on you." Bayla examines me, and I squirm under her gaze. We've never been super close, but we'd always gotten along until recently. Lately, she's been sick of me and not afraid of saying so. "You look different tonight," she says slowly.

"I think so too," I admit. "This might be my year."

Bayla snorts. "Sixth grade? Sixth grade is *no one's* year," she says. "It's the most awful, difficult year you'll ever have. You've just got to get through it." She shrugs and looks suddenly wry. "Of course, tenth grade has kind of been a nightmare too, so I guess it can get worse."

"It seems really hard," I offer.

Bayla heaves a sigh. "It's *miserable*," she says. "I don't think I've stopped studying since I started school. But that's what the honors classes are like. If you don't keep up, you fall behind."

"Ew," I say, trying to imagine it. There are no tracked classes until next year, when math will have us split up. "I'm glad I'll never be in an honors class. Much too much pressure."

Bayla scoffs. "You could easily do honors if you put yourself into it. It isn't easy for me either," she points out. "But it's just a matter of how much time you're willing to spend on schoolwork every night." Her eyes glimmer with sudden amusement. "Of course, more time on school would mean much less time running off with Gayil Itzhaki, so I don't think there's a chance for you."

I stare at her. "You *know?*" No one knows. I go out to roller-blade and come back a little while later with none the wiser. Bayla is always buried in homework, and there's no way—

"Our window looks out at the side yard," Bayla says, sitting back against the couch and looking smug. "I take breaks, you know. I've seen the two of you sneaking out a few times. What's that all about? You and the class queen?"

"That's not a *thing*," I say, tossing a throw pillow at Bayla. "She's just popular."

Bayla's eyebrows rise. "How nice for her. How's that working out for you?"

"We're doing something together." I shift in my seat, relieved to have someone to talk to about all of this. Ema is out at shul, and the house is empty. Telling Bayla is safe, safer than talking to anyone else about it, and I'm careful what I reveal. "Just little pranks to shake up the class a little. We swapped everyone's notebooks one day. And did a thing with slime another."

"Whoa." Bayla eyes me speculatively. "I thought your class was supposed to be, like, a bunch of angels. And isn't Gayil the school poster child?" She puts her hands on her lap, demure and mocking, and bats her eyelashes at me. "Oh, *Morah*, I have such problems! I wanted to visit nursing home residents tonight but it might inter-fere with the amount of time I spend studying, and I don't know if I'll get *all* the extra credit—"

"Shut up." I throw another pillow at her. She sends the first back to me, and I toss another one at her. "Gayil isn't *fake*. She's not per-fect either." I think about the way that she'd inadvertently hurt Rena, that first prank. "She makes mistakes. But she's a good person.

She taught me how to rollerblade," I say, and I feel that jolt of pride at it. I bet I'm the only one who can say *that*, and half the class would be envious of me if they knew. I might be invisible, but I'm not invisible to Gayil, and that matters more than anything. "And she's the first person in school who's noticed I exist in years, so——"

"Okay, okay," Bayla says, holding up her hands. "I got it. I'm just too cynical for my own good." She offers me a dimpled grin. "Kind of cool, being secret friends with someone like Gayil, huh?" Bayla has friends—she's smart and sarcastic and her teacher last year called her *a force to be reckoned with* on her report card—but Goodmans don't have the leader gene. We're staid and we work hard and we stay out of trouble, most of the time, and that's enough for us to fit in fine in Fairview, just like everyone else.

People like Gayil though . . . they're destined to shine. And I glow a little too, in Gayil's sunbeams.

I see her again the next day, on my way back from shul. Most of the seven shuls in our development were once houses, but a few are boxy buildings in the inner U of the neighborhood. The words of our prayers vary minimally from shul to shul, but each davening experience is all about other things: the cadence of the singing, the speed at which prayers are read, the number of children there, or the length of the rabbi's speech. We don't go to any of them. Our shul is in the preschool next to Fairview Bais Yaakov, and I usually linger outside, standing close to groups of girls my age and trying to break into conversations.

Today, it feels silly to try to do that. I have a friend now, maybe two, and I don't need to do that uncomfortable bit where I try to talk, get cut off, and let my voice trail off. Instead, I lean against the outer wall of the shul and try to daven a little bit, and a few girls drift over to stand beside me and daven. We all file inside for shofar blowing, and I have to bite back a laugh when the blower makes a strangled kind of burping noise on his first attempt. A girl catches my eye, both of us with lips twitching, and we wander outside together again after.

None of my classmates are at my shul, but I still feel a little less invisible today, and I even dare to wave at Gayil when I catch sight of her, herding along four of her younger siblings. All the Itzhaki kids have the same bend to their nose, the same light brown skin and glittering smiles, though none of them quite compare to Gayil. A few of them wave madly back at me, and Gayil falls into step with me as we head back to our houses. Ema looks surprised and Bayla takes her arm, helping her hang back as I move into the Itzhaki crowd. "Shul was *long*," I say, mostly to make conversation.

"Not ours," Gayil says brightly. "We finished a half hour ago and then ate cake. I'm stuffed."

"I'm not hungry either," I say quickly, at once self-conscious about my weight.

Gayil eyes me dubiously. "You must be," she says. "It's been *hours*." She pats her stomach. "I don't think I would have made it home without cake, and it's literally down the block."

I laugh. Gayil is pulled away by little Aharon, who is squabbling with Rikki, and I hold Eitan's hand as we cross the crowded street. The Itzhakis are a *lot*, and I've always been overwhelmed by them, but today I'm feeling bold. "Hey," I say as we near our houses. "If you wanted to come by after your meal, it's nice and quiet at my house."

Gayil looks startled, then thoughtful. She nods slowly. "I'll see you then," she says, and it makes me want to shout, to sing it out to the world. I've been following Gayil for a week, but this is different. This is *me*, making the first move. This has nothing to do with pranks or school.

It's just Gayil and me, hanging out, just the way that friends do.

CHAPTER 10

Gayil pokes her head into my bedroom a little after our meal has ended, looking breathless and flushed from her own meal and holding a large swirl lollipop. "We had extras," she says, and she slips into the room and slides onto my floor as though she's been here a dozen times.

I look around, suddenly self-conscious. There are still some stuffed animals on my shelf, and some non-Jewish fantasy books that I'd gotten from the library for the holidays. I notice for the first time that there are spots where the carpet is worn, and the bunk bed has a few sagging parts that I'd never noticed until today. It's not a room that would attract someone like Gayil.

But she leans her head against the flaking yellow paint and says, "It is *so* nice to be somewhere quiet. Shlomit wouldn't let go of me for the whole meal, which is a pain when you're trying to wash dishes." She holds up her dress to show me the wet stains on it. "And Bracha ditched me to go to a friend, so I did all the cleanup alone. I wanted my mother to get a little nap in." She smiles sheepishly, and I think that Bayla would probably laugh at me now for insisting that Gayil is anything but perfect.

"You're so *good*," I say instead. "I didn't wash anything." I roll my eyes. "My mother obsessively reuses aluminum foil pans, so she spends an hour after the meal cleaning out each one and checking for holes. It's so silly. They're, like, *thirty cents each*."

Gayil looks astonished. "My mother does that too! She doesn't check for holes though." She gives me an aggrieved sigh. "She once put a pan of potato kugel in the oven and it leaked like fungus through the bottom of the pan. It was *gross*. And a little cool," she admits, flashing me that gleaming white smile. "Science project gone very wrong."

She gets up, wandering around the room as she talks. "Oh, I used to have this bear. We got it from our kindergarten teacher, right?" She pauses at the books, and I tense. Other kids read a lot of non-Jewish books—I see them at the library all the time—but I can't imagine anyone in my class admitting to enjoying them. We're the perfect Bais Yaakov girls, and we'd never expose ourselves to anything *non-Jewish*. "My sister *loves Keeper of the Lost Cities*," Gayil says, holding up one of the books. "I don't think she's up to this one yet."

I can't believe it. "She can borrow it if she gets to it before Rosh Hashanah is over," I offer. "I've read it a bunch of times already."

"I'm not a fantasy kind of person," Gayil admits, and she lowers her voice. "I actually like reading those big illustrated books about space and the ocean. Sometimes biographies. I know it's *weird*, but I just don't have the kind of imagination for these kinds of books. I'm not a dreamer like you." She flashes me another smile, a little more tentative, and sinks to the floor again.

I've never thought of myself as a dreamer, but as Gayil says it, I can see how it suits me. I'm always thinking about what might be—what will happen next, what could happen instead, what I can do to change things—and maybe that makes me a dreamer. I've always just thought that I was missing so much that I could only see that.

"You have plenty of imagination," I think to point out. "You came up with all the pranks."

"We should do another one tomorrow night," Gayil says, already contemplating it. "I have to figure out the logistics, but I have something in mind." There is a sudden edge to her voice, and I wonder if I've upset her by bringing it up. Maybe she doesn't want to dwell on pranks on a day like Rosh Hashanah.

I watch her in silence, a little cowed by the sharpness that emerged, and Gayil looks at me, and then exhales. "There's such a *stillness* here," she says, changing the topic as though we'd never been talking about the pranks. "I feel like everything else in my life is moving so fast, and the world just . . . *stops* right here."

It is factual, not quite warm but not angry either, and I relax. "This is it," I say lightly. "The most boring place in the world. Shaindy Goodman's bedroom."

Gayil scoffs. "Not boring," she says, and she tilts her head and looks at me. "You aren't at all like I thought you would be," she murmurs, and there is a quiet note to her voice, a tinge of regret that I don't understand.

I laugh, uncomfortable. "You can't tell me that you thought I'd be anything," I say. "No one *thinks* about me. I'm invisible, remember?"

Gayil regards me steadily. "Not to me," she says, and she tugs something out from the sleeve of her dress. It's her charm bracelet, and today it sports a simple charm, one I've never seen her wear before. An apple, for Rosh Hashanah. "Take it," she says suddenly, unclasping the charm. "So whenever you feel that way, you'll remember that I see you."

I gape at her, flabbergasted at her sudden kindness. "I can't take it," I say, but Gayil still watches me, expectant. "It's yours."

She tilts her head. "Then let me take yours," she says, and she reaches up to the windowsill above our heads and slides my charm bracelet down from where I'd left it before Rosh Hashanah. She holds it out to me, the silvery *S* dangling from it, and I hesitate. My parents had gotten me the *S*, and it had been a special gift, one that I don't think that they'd appreciate me trading away.

But this is different. This is Gayil, offering me something I've wanted more than charm bracelets and Heelys, offering me the elusive magic that keeps every girl our age going. To be *seen*. To be *known*. To have a *friend*.

I unclasp the *S* and put it in her palm. Gayil holds it, attaches it to her own bracelet, and tucks it back under her sleeve. "Who are you?" she asks, peering at me, and I have no answer for her, other than *invisible*.

There is also *dreamer* now, also *sneaky*, also *friend*. I am picking up aspects so quickly that I hardly know who I am anymore. I think back to this morning, to standing in shul without struggling to melt into other people, and I don't know who I am. "You know what I think?" Gayil murmurs. "I think you're so obsessed with what people think of you that you never really let yourself be a person." She laughs, a careless dismissal of her own words. "Meanwhile, I'm just trying to be remembered."

"Everyone will remember you." It's the obvious response. She's *Gayil*, and she's unforgettable.

"Not everyone. Not when it matters," Gayil whispers, and there is a dark cast to her face. She shakes it away, her fingers toying with the *S* charm that pokes out of her sleeve. "I have nine siblings," she says, and it's self-effacing. "I'm one of a horde of Fairview kinderlach. The only people I can count on to remember me are my friends. My friends are my *life*," she says. She is speaking to someone else, has a face shrouded in shadow, and she looks like someone I've never seen before.

The room feels a little cooler, the sky a little darker, and I shiver and then reject the sheer absurdity of what Gayil is saying. "You have no idea," I say, and it's bitter, angry in a way I don't let myself be. I can't be angry. Anger isn't *Bais Yaakov*, isn't fair, isn't the way that we're meant to compose ourselves. Anger is messy and wrong when there's no one to be angry at, and it's not right for me to direct it at Gayil, who doesn't deserve it for being everything I'm not. "You don't know what it's like to be alone."

Gayil laughs, harsh and rough. "I know more than you'd think," she says, and something on her face frightens me, has all of my instincts screaming at me to run.

I don't run. I wait, and Gayil collects herself. "Nothing scares me more than being alone," she says, her voice unsteady. It grows firmer, finds that sweet and spirited polish that makes Gayil so special. "I'm not like you, Shaindy," Gayil says. "You're *good* alone. You know how to make it work for you. Me . . . I feel like I'm always on the balance beam, teetering, and everyone's just . . . standing around me, waiting for me to slip up. Waiting for me to be brought back down to earth, no matter the cost."

She sounds distant again, and I shift guiltily. Have I ever felt that way about Gayil? Not in the past week, when we've been building a friendship. But maybe before. Maybe there had been some savage part of me that had been smug when Gayil had gotten questions wrong in class or had missed the ball during a machanayim game. In the summer, I'd lamented it more than once—had watched Gayil stroll into a bunkhouse of fifteen girls, eight of them strangers, and win over every single one.

Gayil is the pinnacle, the girl who everyone strives to become. But to become Gayil, you'd have to tear down Gayil first, and she lives her life acutely aware of it.

Boo hoo, a mean little part of me thinks, maybe in Bayla's voice. *Stinks to be perfect.* Gayil has no idea what it's like for the rest of us, where we don't have anything to be afraid of losing, and I almost want to tell her—

Except that now I do have something that I'm terrified of losing. And if I throw myself a pity party right now, after that *something . . . someone* has opened up to me, I'll lose her for good.

I say, "I don't think like that," and Gayil gives me a smile unlike any she's given me before, wide and bright and pretty. There is something else to it though: something that makes my skin crawl for no discernible reason.

It isn't until later that I finally realize what it is.

Gayil's smile hadn't reached her eyes at all.

CHAPTER 11

We meet up after Rosh Hashanah, late on Sunday night. We have school tomorrow for half a day. Some girls have already had their Bas Mitzvahs and are fasting for what our teachers call Tzom Gedaliah and what we call day-after-Rosh-Hashanah bloat, but I don't have to worry about that yet. My birthday isn't for months, and I'm only going to fast on Yom Kippur for practice.

Gayil is fasting tomorrow, so she eats a candy bar in front of her house while she waits for me, a folder tucked under her arm. I fasten my Rollerblades and we fall into step together, gliding down the block. I'm getting faster, enough that I have to control my speed so I don't pull ahead, and Gayil says admiringly, "You're getting *good.* You'll have those Heelys any day."

"We're going to order them this week," I tell her. Ema had been proud when she'd seen me on my Rollerblades, beaming with that shimmering smile that she gets when I've done something unexpected. "So I'll have them for Succos, when everyone's outside." I glance at her wrist, curious, and I see that she's wearing my *S* on it. I'm wearing her apple, its silvery color gleaming in the street lights, and I pinch it between my fingers and let it go. "What are we up to today?"

We shouldn't have to worry about anyone being at the school tonight, after Rosh Hashanah. It's empty on the block, and the playground gate is still propped open from all the kids who'd played there during the holiday. Today though, it all feels different. The thin crescent moon overhead gives little light, and there is none filtering in from the high school across the street. Every movement in the wind feels like someone is watching us, and I shiver and twist whenever something shifts in the corner of my eye.

Gayil scans the fob against the metal lock, and we slip inside. It's dark in the building, the lights all out and the silence oppressive. I take my Rollerblades off, and Gayil slides the wheels back into her Heelys, and we tiptoe up the stairs. Gayil speaks in a whisper. "Something small today," she says. "I was thinking about the tests that Morah Neuman puts into her desk drawer to grade while we work on the Succos projects. Last week we had the quiz on Rosh Hashanah, right? I thought it might be funny to submit a new one for the teacher's pet. Really confuse Morah Neuman."

She holds the folder out to me in the dark. There is a single dim light in the hallway upstairs, and I open the folder near it, scanning the answers.

They're supposed to be funny, I guess. The questions aren't on the paper. Morah Neuman had read them to us, and we'd numbered our answers and submitted them on a plain piece of paper. A number of them are right, but others have been changed. I remember that the third had been *What is another name for Rosh Hashanah?* and Gayil's doctored paper says, *Morah Neuman Appreciation Day.* Other answers are less fawning and downright disrespectful. One of them just says, *I don't care, I know you don't grade these anyway,* and another is *Rosh Hashanah exists to give us a break from your classroom.*

But the most alarming thing about the paper is the name that Gayil has written at the top of it, clear and in a handwriting that is surprisingly similar to the girl's actual handwriting. "Tzivia Krasner," I read, and my stomach plummets. "Why Tzivia?"

Gayil shrugs, "She's the last person *alive* who'd snap like this," she says dismissively. "I don't want someone getting in trouble for it. I just want to have fun."

It sounds reasonable when Gayil says it like that, but I still feel that sick sensation in my stomach. Gayil had *worked* on this, had gotten Tzivia's handwriting and mimicked it pretty well, and Tzivia is . . . maybe a friend. Maybe just someone who looks out for me when so few people have noticed me. Tzivia doesn't like Gayil, and she wouldn't appreciate being the butt of her joke.

"I can't do this to Tzivia," I say, chewing on my lip. "She's . . . she's my *friend.* And if Morah Neuman does blame her—"

"She won't," Gayil says confidently. "Why would anyone believe that Tzivia would do something like this? It'll be funny. It'll be another mystery—"

"It's almost Yom Kippur," I try, though I don't know if it will change anything. We've spent a month of school being told about teshuva, about changing and making amends, and at this point, we're so inundated with reminders to *be better* that it's easy to let them wash over us. "Is this really the time?"

"It's the perfect time," Gayil says, still stubborn with her certainty. "It's not an *attack,* Shaindy. It's just a joke."

"She's my friend," I say again, and I am nauseated with it.

Gayil turns to face me, those blazing eyes hooded in the dim light. "And what am I, then?" she demands. "What are we?"

I freeze, caught under the glare of Gayil's expectations. What are we? I don't know, but I do know that her charm is lying against my wrist, and she's the one I find every night, waiting for me. I know that she's not just aspirational—I don't just want to *be* Gayil, I want to be *hers*. I want to belong to Gayil like Devorah and Rena do, to be her friend outside the cover of night, and if this is a test, then I'm failing it.

"I can't," I say, helpless, and I think about Tzivia, who had been the only one in camp to notice me. We'd sat next to each other during meals and she'd been the first one who'd followed me on that one, shining day when I'd been the leader of our little group. Tzivia is quiet and thoughtful and kind, and this feels like a betrayal of her, even if it doesn't get her in trouble.

I am nothing if not loyal to the rare people who reach out to me, and I waver in place, torn. Gayil makes a noise of disgust. "*Whatever*," she says, and she takes the paper from me, smooths it out again, and stalks away from the light toward our classroom. I follow her to it, trailing back, and Gayil pushes the door to the classroom open—

"*Wait!*" I hiss, catching sight of something on the desk.

Gayil pauses, turning to look back at me. I can't see her eyes in the dark, don't know what she's thinking, but I whisper, "Is that a bear on the desk?"

"A bear?" she echoes, her voice as low as mine. She opens the door another crack, and we can see it clearly now. There *is* a bear on the desk, a stuffed one that's sitting there as though it belongs, and I watch it with grim foreboding. I've seen one of these before.

"My downstairs neighbor has one of those because she has a babysitting service come every day," I say, pulling Gayil back from the door. She stares at it, still uncomprehending, and I whisper, "There's a camera inside it. It records everything that happens in a room. Morah Neuman must have put it there to catch us." I feel the wash of relief, the certainty that this is my way out of this mess. Tzivia is going to be fine. "You can't go in there. She'll know."

Gayil stares at the desk, then back at me. "Not if I do this right," she breathes, her voice barely audible. "Watch me." And she drops to the ground.

I don't want to help her. I don't want to do this to Tzivia. I don't even understand why Gayil is so set on doing all of these pranks when they haven't done anything to cheer up our class. But I can't let Gayil get caught either. Caught between two friends, I step back and refuse to do a thing. But I do watch her in silence, keeping a cautious eye on the teddy bear camera as Gayil slithers across the floor. She stays against the wall, sliding along the corner behind the teacher's desk, and she only sits up when she's finally in front of the drawer where Morah Neuman keeps the tests. Carefully, she pulls out Morah Neuman's folder and rifles through it, taking out Tzivia's old test and putting in her replacement. She crumples the paper into a ball and slithers back to me, and I edge the door open a little more and try my best to hide behind it.

I'm struck by a song that we used to sing in preschool at this time of year, a reminder to be better. In English, it translates to something eerie. *An eye sees, an ear listens, and all your deeds will be written.* The teddy bear watches and listens, and I do nothing at all to stop Gayil.

"We did it," Gayil says, carefully shutting the door. Her voice sounds lighter now, relieved, and she reaches out and squeezes my hand. "You make a *great* lookout," she says, and there is no more of the anger from before in her voice. She tucks the crumpled paper into the pocket of her sweatshirt and we head downstairs.

Abruptly, my decision to refuse to participate feels like I'd made another, worse decision, one that had betrayed Tzivia. I twitch, the discomfort sticking in my throat. "I didn't . . ." I start, determined to hold on to what I'd *meant* to do, how I'd meant not to hurt Tzivia, but Gayil is already ahead of me, her shoes' wheels popped out as she rolls down the hallway.

I put my Rollerblades back on at the bottom of the steps, that sour taste of betrayal lingering in my mouth. I'm still sure that we can't be entirely alone out here. But there is no one watching us, no movements in the building, and we slip away again without a trace, Gayil leading the way back home.

CHAPTER 12

The next morning is quiet, Fairview emerging slowly from the sleepy haze that comes along with every holiday. Kids who go to schools farther out linger at corners, quiet and glum faced, and even the usual rush of kids through the development on their way to school feels more muted than usual. I'm lacing my Rollerblades when I see Rena and Devorah roll up to the house next to mine, and a gloomy-eyed Gayil emerges.

"Morning is the *worst*," she says. "We need a full day to recover from Rosh Hashanah."

"We'll have this afternoon," Rena says, running a hand through her short hair. "Want to go out to the shopping center and pick out clothes for Succos?"

Gayil looks even gloomier. "This is my first fast," she says. "I'm not going anywhere when I get home. I'll just collapse on the couch and read until it's over."

I straighten, finished eavesdropping, and I rollerblade down the street just as they leave Gayil's porch. I contemplate them, the cool touch of the apple charm against my skin giving me courage I've never possessed before, and I say, "Hey, guys."

Gayil gives me a sharp, warning look. I remember *What are we?* and her eyes on me, and my heart beats a groove against my chest.

But Rena looks startled but not unfriendly, and she says, "Hey, Shaindy." Devorah gives a little wave.

Gayil speeds up, moving faster than I am, and her friends keep up. I hang back, my heart sinking, and I recognize the reprimand for what it is. I can't blow our cover. We can't even acknowledge each other in school. Not now. Not while we're still doing these pranks.

Gayil's distance makes perfect sense when she talks about it to me, when we're together and she's giving me her full attention. When she isn't, I feel a creeping despondency, a shame that burns at my throat and makes my eyes water up. Sometimes, it's even worse than it had been before, when I hadn't tasted what it might mean to be friends with someone like Gayil.

And I know that someday, the pranks are going to end. And when that happens—when Gayil gets bored or the school changes the locks or *something* changes—then, there's nothing standing in our way. There's no reason for Gayil to ignore me.

And she won't, right? She *likes* me. She's said that I'm nothing like she'd imagined. I have to believe that I'm not just a secret friend but a real one, that I'm not someone she's embarrassed to be seen with.

If I don't believe that, I think I might shatter. Not all at once, like a glass to the floor, but in slow pieces, falling one at a time to hard ground, until there is nothing left of me but a few jagged bits with a shape I don't recognize. I touch the apple charm, a tangible reminder of what I mean to Gayil, and I glide down the block with my eyes fixed on Gayil's back.

In school, Tzivia smiles at me when she sees me, a vague tension still in her eyes from our kind of argument on Friday. I feel a wave of guilt, remembering what I'd stood by and let happen last night, and I say, "Hey, Tzivia. How was your Rosh Hashanah?"

She looks relieved and opens her mouth to respond when Morah Neuman bustles by, clearly pleased at the lack of chaos in the hallway so far. "Let's go, girls! We have a lot to do and not much time to do it. In, in, in—" The waves of her straw-yellow wig bounce as she moves, the faint smell of sickly-sweet perfume wafting past with it, and she directs us forward, into the room.

We bury ourselves in the happy monotony of our Succos projects, sticking pins through sequins and affixing them to the boards. I glance at my project for the first time since the weekend with fresh eyes, noting with pleased surprise that my big plan for iridescent swirls has worked. The pattern seems to gleam with multicolored pastels, and when I tilt it just so, it hits the light of the sun through the window and glitters.

"That looks so cool," Tzivia whispers, and she earns a warning glance from Morah Neuman as we work. I admire my board for another minute before I return to the sequins that spell out the Hebrew words on the decoration, and Morah Neuman turns back to the rest of the class as she speaks.

"Rosh Hashanah is considered the Day of Judgment, when we are each judged for all our actions for the past year," she says. "The good and the bad—it's all weighted, and we are categorized. Are we good? Are we evil? Or are we in between both?"

"We're all in between," Rena says.

Morah Neuman nods. "So we move forward," she says, "And we go from judgment to atonement. Yom Kippur is the day to atone.

Most of you will be fasting, and most of you will spend the day in shul, reliving your worst actions in the past year and how you might make them right." She clears her throat. "Think of the worst thing you've done in the past year."

At first, I draw a blank. I think about Rena's hair, about Tzivia's test, about every fight I've had with Bayla, but all of that feels different, unintentional or something I'd slipped into thoughtlessly. I hadn't done it to hurt anyone.

And then, my mind drifts to another moment, a few weeks before this school year had started. It hadn't been *bad*, really, not how it had turned out, but I can remember the shameful, awful intentions behind it, the resentment I'd felt that had made me seize a chance to shine. I don't think too hard about it, don't let myself get lost in the moment—the hilly green spot in the middle of the mountains, the squat bunkhouses on either side of us, the eyes of other girls' expectant on me like never before—and I stop myself from dwelling too much on what had happened. I close my eyes, and I listen to Morah Neuman.

"And now, the four stages we've discussed. Are you still doing it?" *Never again*, I think silently. "Have you admitted it aloud?" I refuse to think about the answer to that. "Do you regret it? Will you do it again?" *Yes. No.*

Morah Neuman says gently, "And remember, even the most heartfelt regret can't undo what an apology can." My eyes snap open, and I stare at her in chagrin. I'm not *apologizing* for that. No one even knows that I'd thought of it that way. Unbidden, my eyes flicker to Gayil, who is watching Morah Neuman with her eyes narrowed. She looks almost angry, and I look uneasily at her. Then Devorah nudges Gayil, and the expression slides smoothly off her face as though it had never been there, replaced with attentiveness.

"Let's try something else," Morah Neuman says. "Think about something good that you've done this year—the best thing that you've done." I can't think of anything at first. My thoughts of good deeds are all limited to *watched the baby downstairs for an hour* and *helped cook for Shabbos*, nothing worth celebrating. I haven't pulled anyone out of burning buildings or solved world hunger. I've just lived my life and tried to do the right thing, some of the time.

"How can you repeat that?" Morah Neuman says. "How can you capture the motivation you felt then and do that again?" She goes on, absentmindedly pulling her test folder from the desk drawer, and I stop listening. Instead, I glance once toward the front of the room and then bury myself in my project, my face burning.

Morah Neuman grades absentmindedly, the lesson petering out, and my classmates murmur to each other around the room as she falls silent. I can hear the whisper of papers being flipped over and left on the other side of the desk, the grinding noise of a pen making check marks against the papers on the hard surface, the low rumble of whispers through the room, and I am at once sure that this is the worst thing that I've done. Betraying Tzivia like this for a practical joke is—

Morah Neuman's pen stops moving. I stare at the letter mem that I'm pinning sequins into, feel my heart pounding, and I think, *this is it*. But maybe it isn't. Maybe Morah Neuman had just absent-mindedly given Tzivia the hundred that she always gets, hadn't even looked at her answers at all, and we're okay. Maybe—

"Tzivia," Morah Neuman says, her voice terse. "Please join me in the hallway."

I look up. Tzivia's eyes are wide, her face ashen, and she looks terrified. She walks slowly, dragging her feet as she maneuvers between desks, and her breath comes in quick, audible sucks. I sink into my seat, avoiding her stare, and I want to cry.

I'd done this. I should have taken the fake test from Gayil and ripped it to shreds, should have warned Morah Neuman, should have kept Tzivia *out of this*. Instead, I listen to muffled voices in the hallway, loud enough for most of the class to hear.

"—the one causing all the trouble in class?" Morah Neuman asks, and I feel even worse.

Tzivia's voice isn't audible, and Morah Neuman says, a little gentler, "—thought your answers indicated someone who is—" I can't make out what she says next.

I do hear Tzivia this time, loud and strident. "I didn't write that!" she says, and the rest of the class looks at each other, uneasy.

"I am so *sick* of this," Tammy declares suddenly. "It's like the whole class is haunted." She glances over at Sheva, the two of them grim with it, and Tammy says, "Well, I'm done. I'm not going to sit around all day waiting to see what this *person* does next." She stands up and does a defiant cartwheel.

I don't know how a cartwheel can be *defiant*, but somehow, Tammy's is. She stands in front of the room, her eyes moving from girl to girl, and she says, "It's time to start asking questions. You're all suspects."

"So are you," Rena points out. "*I'm* the only one who isn't." She touches her short hair and glares around the class. "I think we should interrogate every girl. Demand answers. Push until we find the guilty person." She looks around the classroom. "Twenty-six girls. Some-one is doing this."

Gayil speaks, and I'm not surprised when she sounds utterly convincing. "I think we should start with *how*," she says. "Someone is coming into school early to do these things. The bees in the classroom? The mixed-up notebooks? How are they getting in?"

Tammy's eyes land on Chana Leah, whose mother works in the school. "Not me," Chana Leah protests. "I wasn't even *in* school on the day with the bees."

"Because you didn't want to be in the classroom when they escaped," Sari points out, her voice loud enough to attract Morah Neuman's attention, and the door opens again.

"No," Chana Leah says, outraged, "Because I had *strep*! You can ask my mother. I was *asleep* when school started!"

"Girls," Morah Neuman says, commanding. She is tall enough that we are awed by her, that the class falls silent when she speaks, and she looks from girl to girl and shakes her head. "You know what?" she says. "You're all right. We're going to get to the bottom of this. Not today," she adds hastily, looking around in reproof. "We've lost enough time today. Tomorrow, I want you all to daven at home and come to the auditorium when school starts. I want to talk to you each one at a time."

I swallow and do my best to hide it. It doesn't matter. No one's looking at me. Rena looks smug, Tammy angry and determined, Devorah amused by the whole thing. Gayil has a set smile on her face, the expression of someone who is just as ready for this thing to be over, and not suspicious at all.

And Tzivia doesn't come back to class until much later.

CHAPTER 13

T zivia finally returns to class when Hebrew is almost over, her face drawn and her eyes red. The day passes in a dream-like daze, my thoughts all rushing over each other in a quest to emerge. I'm sure that I'll be implicated tomorrow. There's no way that Morah Neuman won't see right through me. I'm going to be kicked out of school, or suspended, and become the class pariah. All the girls who have always tolerated me or been half-heartedly nice will now have reason to resent me, to hate me, to push me away. If I've been lonely in my class until now, it'll be *nothing* compared to how I feel once everyone despises me.

And I won't have Gayil anymore either, I realize with a rush of grief. Gayil will ace Morah Neuman's interrogation without arousing any suspicions, and she won't be able to talk to me anymore, or she'll seem guilty by association. I'm going to lose *everything,* and I hadn't even realized I'd had much to lose.

I watch Gayil during lunch, see her sitting at her table with Rena and Devorah, their heads together as they discuss the big drama that is sure to unravel tomorrow. I'm sitting at a table with Miri, Sari, and Ariella, who haven't acknowledged me at all. "I hope they find the girl behind it soon," Sari says, shuddering. "I could have *died* if a bee had stung me. My mother didn't even want me to go back to school."

Ariella unwraps her sandwich with one hand, her long fingers drumming against the table as she eats it. "I can't believe that the school has let it go on for so long. I bet they install cameras in every classroom now."

Miri snorts. "They don't have the money for that. My old school—Bais Torah Fairview—only got cameras because they applied for some security grant. What are they going to say to get them here? A girl is stealing people's notebooks and giving them back to the wrong people?"

I glance away from them, desperate to avoid the conversation, then I get up to wash my hands, taking my food with me. There aren't many open seats in the lunchroom by now, not unless I sit with strangers, and I hesitate, looking around, until I catch Tzivia's eye.

She still looks upset, but she pats the spot beside her, and I sit with trepidation. Chana Leah and Temima are sitting opposite her, and they're talking about the pranks too. "I had nothing to do with them," Chana Leah says, still caught up in the accusations. "*Nothing*. Why would I want to hurt Rena? She's so nice."

"Sometimes," Temima says, sniffling into a tissue. "Sometimes you kind of get the feeling that she thinks she's above it all." She shrugs. "Devorah is nice. Rena and Gayil though . . ."

Tzivia interjects gently, her words measured. "It's right before Yom Kippur," she says, and the other two girls look shamefaced. "Trust me," she adds, her face grim. "No one wants to find out who's behind this like I do. You should have seen what the girl wrote on that paper, pretending to be me."

"What did the handwriting look like?" Chana Leah wants to know. "Couldn't Morah Neuman compare it to the rest of the class's?"

Tzivia shrugs. "It looked like *mine*," she says. "Not perfectly, but the writer tried to make the *t*'s like I do, with the curve at the bottom, and the line through the seven. It wasn't just a joke with my name on it. It was *nasty*. Like the girl had it in for me."

She looks to me for support, and I feel suddenly defensive, protective of the pranks that have been only meant to lighten up the class. "I'm sure she didn't," I say. "I mean, these are really just *pranks*, you know? Silly little things designed to be funny."

Tzivia scoffs. "No, they aren't," she says. "Look at them. Think about them. Every single one of the pranks was targeted toward someone in the class." She sits back grimly, her face set. "Someone has a grudge, and she's taking it out on us."

I shrug, noncommittal, and the other girls' attention drifts away from me, as it always does. They return to safer topics, like what they're doing for Succos vacation, and I eat my lunch and think about what Tzivia has said.

She's wrong. She has to be. These are just pranks, most of them affecting the whole class, except for this one and the first. And Gayil doesn't have it in for *Rena*, her best friend. That would be ridiculous.

But there is something that niggles at me, something that rings true about Tzivia's suspicions. Gayil has an agenda. She *has* to, because why else is all of this going on? Why would she keep it up when the class is angry and afraid instead of enjoying the pranks? When the school is fed up with them enough to hunt down the perpetrator?

I watch Gayil for the rest of the day. She talks with her friends, breezy and unworried, and she shows no sign of malice. I wonder, why Rena and not Devorah? Why would she target the friend who *loves* her hair more than anything? Devorah's hair is long and blonde, pretty enough, but Rena's curls had been her point of pride, an obsession that the whole class had known about.

Tzivia. Rena. Who else had been directly affected by the pranks? Sheva had been upset about a missing notebook, I remember, but that sounds more like an unfortunate coincidence. Her school notebook had been there, hadn't it? In my mind, I try to list the girls who had shrieked the loudest when the bees had been released. Temima? Chana Leah? Hudi?

There is no discernible pattern in the girls Gayil had chosen. Her targets are random, spanning different groups of friends and different kinds of girls. They have nothing in common beyond being in the class, and I want to doubt Tzivia's words.

I want to, but I can't.

I doodle names and make lines between them, connecting girls to each other. Rena and Tzivia are both top students, but Meira does just as well as them, maybe even better than Rena, and none of the pranks had touched her. She'd been one of the last to leave when the bees had emerged from the closet. Devorah has been untouched, and Sheva is only a question mark, a maybe target who makes no sense either. Everyone likes Sheva. She's nice and she keeps to herself, sticking with Tammy but friendly with plenty of other girls.

Then again, I'd thought that everyone had liked Gayil until Tzivia had proven otherwise. I'm on the outskirts of the class, the last person to fully grasp the dynamics in the classroom. Maybe I've missed some tension.

I make a line between all three and connect it to a little question mark above a sketch of a bee. I just don't know. I'll ask Gayil about Sheva's notebook later and see how she reacts. Gayil is hard to read, but I'm beginning to get the hang of it. She lets me see a part of her that I don't know if even her friends have noticed, and I suspect it might be the key to understanding her motivations.

By the end of the school day, I have a web of names and lines, connecting groups of girls and making notes next to their names. I watch Gayil carefully as she packs up for the day, leaning against the locker on Rena's other side. Is there a difference in how she speaks to Rena and how she speaks to Devorah? I can't place it.

No. There is something. The laughter with Rena sounds more strained, the smile on her face more pronounced—as though she is putting it on herself. With Devorah, she is calmer, in control and content. With Rena, she's pretending.

Then there *had* been something malicious in her target, unless I'm imagining the whole thing.

I trail behind them on the way home, watching their body language too. They're all on Heelys, gliding down the street, but Gayil moves closer to Devorah, avoids lingering too close to Rena. Rena must notice, because she doesn't try to bridge that gap. Instead, she calls to them as though this is normal and keeps her distance from Gayil. I see a flash of frustration—of *confusion* in her eyes as she says goodbye to Gayil, and I wonder if she doesn't know what she's done either.

I leave my homework on the desk when I get home and I sit cross-legged on the thin carpet of my room, brown and rough and too thin to cushion me well. It's still bright enough outside that I don't have to turn on the light at first, but the sun sets as I stare at the paper, the room darkening around me until I can hardly make out the words. Tzivia. Rena. Sheva. Maybe Sari? She's the one who'd gone home, who'd been allergic to bees. Why these four?

I lean the paper against the metal folding chair that sits at the desk and scribble over Sari's name, because it just leaves me even more confused. Sari is in a completely different group of girls than anyone else here. She's confident and a little quirky, the kind of girl who might have been bullied in a class less welcoming than mine. Her mother had worked in our camp, which had been the only reason she'd gone, and she'd hung on to a tolerant Tammy for most of the month.

None of this makes sense. I tuck the paper into my binder and focus on my homework. Gayil will be here soon. I need to get to work.

CHAPTER 14

Gayil is sitting on the steps of her porch when I come outside, engrossed in a book that she squints at in the dim light of sunset. Her fingers run through her hair, twisting the black locks around them and between them, and she is biting a nail. I hadn't realized that Gayil bites her nails. It's a physical hint of imperfection, and I stare at her, fascinated, until she looks up and smiles. "There you are," she says. "What took you so long?"

"Math," I say truthfully. "I still don't have the hang of fractions."

Gayil makes a face. "Oh, me too."

"Please. I know you aced the first math quiz this year." Everyone knows, because only one girl in the class had gotten full credit *and* the two bonus questions, and Gayil had beamed so widely when she'd gone up to get her quiz that everyone had known who the mystery girl was. We'd all been happy too. It's rare that it's someone other than the three smartest kids in the class, and Gayil is a top five for sure but not quite on Tzivia's level.

Gayil shakes her head. "Right, but now Mrs. Gelman thinks that I know my stuff. I can't slack anymore. Too many expectations."

"I think you worry too much about everyone else's expectations," I say. It's playful, but I mean it. Gayil seems perpetually stressed by what everyone else thinks of her, even more than I do. Maybe because I'm resigned to my fate, and hers is something worth holding on to.

"We can't all be as strong as you, Shaindy," Gayil says, but she sets the book down and seizes my hand, leading me to her backyard. As we move along, the identical lamp sconces at the back of every house on the block snap on, illuminating our path to the trampoline. "Come on. Let's figure out how we're going to handle the interrogation tomorrow." I kick off my Rollerblades and climb up behind her, and I sit opposite her in the middle of the trampoline. "How are you under pressure?"

"Terrible," I say honestly.

Gayil fixes me with a piercing stare, so familiar that it takes me a minute to realize that it feels exactly like Morah Neuman. "Shaindel Goodman," she says in a haughty, proper voice. "Did you have anything to do with the pranks in my classroom?"

I have to stifle a laugh. "No, Morah Itzhaki," I say, pursing my lips. "I had no idea. But I think they're really funny." I remember suddenly that I was going to ask Gayil about the notebook. "Hey, Gayil? You know that Sheva had a second notebook? That one she used to write in at camp. Did we take it out when we were swapping notebooks?"

Gayil shrugs. "No idea. There were a lot of notebooks," she says. Her voice gives nothing away, and I stiffen, suddenly sure that it had, in fact, been intentional. Sheva belongs on the list too.

I stare at Gayil. I don't really know her, definitely not as well as I thought I did. What is she doing? Why did she want me to do this whole scheme with her? Is she just counting on the fact that I'm lonely enough that she knows I'll be loyal to her? Is she right?

She smiles at me, still in character, and she puts on the voice again. "Shaindel," she says again. "I want to know the truth."

"The *truth*," I say, and I watch Gayil's eyes, the flicker of a secret burning within them. She's wearing my charm again, the *S* glinting in the lamplight, and she watches me as if I have something she desperately wants. "The truth is that I spend all night studying, because we're less than a month into school and we're already swamped with work."

Gayil snorts. "Now *that's* convincing. Can you believe we have a Yom Kippur quiz *and* a Succos quiz on Thursday? Just give us the test after vacation when we can study all Succos."

"I do *not* plan on spending my Succos studying," I inform Gayil. "And I think I can guarantee that everyone else feels the same way."

Gayil shrugs. "I wasn't going to study at all," she says, and she grins. "Maybe five minutes at the start of school that day. I have a good memory."

"Lucky you. I don't remember anything for more than a few minutes," I admit. "I couldn't tell you what I had for dinner."

"You had chicken and rice," Gayil says. "I could smell it from outside. We had salmon." She wrinkles her nose. "I slathered it with sauce and spices and it was *still* bad." She climbs to her feet. "Come on."

I'm confused. "Where are we going?"

Gayil grins. "What, you think Morah Neuman can scare us off now? Hang on." She climbs off the trampoline and runs to the back patio, a shadow across the dark lawn, where she has a cloth bag.

Inside it is a container of what looks like dish soap. "It's bubble bath," she says. "When you spill it, the liquid looks clear. But add a little bit of water to it and it'll go wild."

"You want to put it in the hallway," I guess. "So we have to call a custodian when class starts." I climb down the trampoline too, slipping on my Rollerblades. "And what happens when he mops up the spill?"

"I hope they float," Gayil says dreamily. "Imagine them drifting through the air like we're underwater, bubbles everywhere. It'll be so pretty."

"And kind of a pain for the custodians," I point out, but I'm a little relieved. *Custodians* seems vague enough that they'll make my web of girls even less realistic. Gayil might not have a grudge at all. She's just unexpectedly chaotic. "Do you really think that it's a good idea to keep up the pranks tonight? What if this is the one that gets us suspended?"

"We're not getting suspended," Gayil says, waving an airy hand. "For one thing, they'll never find out that it's us. And if they do, they'll never believe it. Sweet, quiet Shaindy and star student Gayil?" She says the description of herself almost mockingly, like it's an imaginary thing she'd dreamed up instead of the truth. "Besides, my father is on the school board. There's no way they'd do anything to me. Maybe give me a stern lecture." She shrugs. "Morah Neuman is just on a power trip. She can't do a thing."

We roll down the street in the goose bumps–raising chill of the night, past older kids and a few who are about our age. They don't look twice at us; there are too many kids in the development to know everyone, and they aren't in our class. The high school yeshiva down the block from Fairview Bais Yaakov is nearly empty, and there's a minivan right by the playground entrance that blocks the view of us as we sneak inside. "Maybe you're right," Gayil says quietly to me. I blink at her, startled to hear those words from her mouth. "Maybe this should be our last prank."

"Until Purim," I suggest. Purim is our upside-down holiday, when pranks are celebrated and classes come up with their own special ones for teachers. Then, Gayil's schemes would be the talk of the class, and no one would get in trouble for them.

Gayil grins at me. "Purim," she agrees, and it sounds like a promise, a reassurance that this isn't the end for us. I cling to it like it's my last hope. "Come on."

She lugs the bag of bubble bath down the hall, and we steal up the stairs, careful in the dark. My Rollerblade laces are hanging loosely from the tips of my pointer fingers, and I trail after Gayil, something niggling at the back of my mind.

It hits me just as Gayil puts her hand on the door out of the stairwell. "Wait," I hiss. "That minivan outside . . . didn't it have a Fairview Bais Yaakov bumper sticker?"

Gayil hesitates, turning to stare at me. "Maybe," she says slowly. "I didn't even notice a car. Why? You think someone's here?"

The stairwell has a long, rectangular window on the door, and we move to it together. I peer into the bottom of the window, Gayil on her tiptoes to look above me, and we squint out into the hall. Our classroom is the first in the hallway, right across from the stairwell, and I think I see something shift in the room.

"It's the light of a phone screen," Gayil whispers, her free hand finding my arm in the dark. "Someone is in there, waiting for us." I can see it now, the shifting phone screen lighting up our darkened classroom. We are frozen by the door of the stairwell, squinting at the light in the room—

And then, with frightening suddenness, a face appears near the door. It's Morah Neuman, her eyes and nose illuminated in eerie angles by the phone, and she peers out at the hallway as we drop away from the window. "That was close," I whisper, crouching by the door. "Let's get out of here."

"No," Gayil says stubbornly. "I won't let her win this round." I can't see her face, but I can imagine it, the thoughtful contemplation that comes with mischief and determination that is so uniquely Gayil Itzhaki. "We're in the wrong place for tomorrow's prank," she says suddenly. "Aren't we?"

I stare at her, uncomprehending, until the meaning of her words finally dawns on me. Tomorrow, we won't be starting our day up here. "Yeah," I say. "We are."

CHAPTER 15

Y ou can't even see the bubble bath in the morning. I'm
almost sure that it's already been cleaned up, because the
floor of the auditorium stage sparkles when we file in
groggily that morning. But there is something electric in the air,
something that pricks our attention as we sit near the stage. Today
is different.

Today, my class is determined to figure out who the secret prank-
sters are.

I stay close to Tzivia, who watches every girl around us with
suspicion. "Sheva's always writing in that notebook," she says,
frowning. "What about Meira? She hates when Rena and I do better than her."

"You didn't start diagramming suspects too, did you?" I ask
playfully.

Tzivia laughs, a surprised little peal. "I did, actually. You too?"

"I read a lot of mysteries," I say truthfully. There aren't a lot of
good Jewish books—they're always kind of similar and I get sick
of them—but the old-school mysteries are pretty good. "I guess I
figured I might have a shot at solving this one."

Tzivia sits on one of the benches arrayed across the auditorium. It's a big room, decorated formally for the shul that uses it on

Shabbos. The walls are a pale brown color, the floor tiled with elaborate diamond patterns, and only the benches are plain, made from hard metal with a fancy wooden finish over the back and the seat. The back of the seat can rotate at a ninety-degree angle to make a long, flat table, but right now, this one is only a bench. At the front of the room is the stage, the curtains open and girls sitting along the steps up to it. No one has gone up there yet, which is good, because the gleaming stage floor is where the bubble bath has been spread.

I try to imagine the bubbles floating off the stage to fill the room. It might be really cool, nice enough that my classmates will appreciate the prank instead of decrying it. Our grand finale might be the prank to finally win them over.

Hopefully, it won't matter at all. Hopefully, I won't flub the questioning today. Morah Neuman sweeps in five minutes late, her eyes sharp as she takes us all in. She looks tired, and I wonder how long she'd spent in the classroom last night, waiting for us. Mrs. Teichman is beside her, equally stern above a businesslike burgundy suit jacket, and I shiver. "We'll call you over one at a time," she says. "Please do not come until you're called. Enjoy your free time—this will replace your morning recess."

No one groans. We're all too nervous to protest. Gayil and I are the only ones who have reason to be worried, but I can see the way that Chana Leah shifts from one foot to the other, how Meira chews on her lip, how Temima sniffles extra loudly, and Tammy seems to jerk from foot to foot with anxious energy. Everyone has a guilty conscience, even though none of them are actually guilty.

Morah Neuman and Mrs. Teichman turn a bench around on the far side of the auditorium, far from the stage, so it faces a second bench. They sit, and Mrs. Teichman calls, "Meira Baum?"

Meira walks slowly to their side of the auditorium, her feet dragging and her head low, and she looks incredibly suspicious to all of us. A murmur fills the auditorium, and Tammy does three nervous cartwheels in front of me, her skirt flying up to reveal colorful non-uniform leggings beneath it.

"Stop," Sheva hisses. "You'll get in trouble." She clenches her jaw, watches Meira worriedly. Meira is sitting with her knees pressed together and her hands folded on her lap, Mrs. Teichman leaning forward to speak to her. She shakes her head and then speaks quickly, and Sheva says, "Do you think she's confessing?"

Silence. Then Meira gets up, walking back to us with a spring in her step, and she's smiling. Mrs. Teichman calls, "Batsheva Cohen?"

Sheva goes, stumbling a little as she makes her way through the auditorium. "It wasn't so bad," Meira says to us. We all gather around her at the base of the stage, hungry for details about what we're about to go through. "Mrs. Teichman just asked me how I feel about the class." She shrugs. "I said the truth: that we're not that kind of class. She agreed with me. Maybe it isn't someone in the classroom at all. Think Morah Neuman has some old student with a grudge?"

"Getting it out of her system before Yom Kippur," Tzivia says ruefully. "Imagine that."

We begin discussing the possibility. By the end, everyone is so convinced that I nearly believe it, and only Gayil is dubious. "How would an old student know Rena's locker combination?" she says. I have no idea why she's being contrary about this. "That seems like something you'd have to see her put in to figure out. And the seventh graders are in the other hallway."

"There are so many girls in the other classes," Rena says, shrugging. "I bet a seventh grader could just slip in next to them and watch me in the hallway without me realizing." She shudders, leaning against the side of the stage. "It's kind of creepy."

One by one, we're called to the principal, and the calm that had settled over each of us is rattled. Every girl might be a suspect, and no one knows if their name is cleared. Gayil is called eighth, and she winds carefully through the benches, moving steadily toward the double doors at the back of the room near where Morah Neuman and Mrs. Teichman wait.

She sits straight with her hands in her lap, and she speaks in that modest, demure way that always wins over the teachers. She's the model Bais Yaakov girl, as always, and no one else looks in her direction. Everyone is positive that she's not guilty.

Everyone except for me, and except for Tzivia, who is watching Gayil with her eyes narrowed from where she sits on the front bench beneath the stage. I wonder what she suspects, and what she might suspect about me too. She's the smartest in the class for a *reason*.

But then Gayil is striding back to us like a soldier returning from war, and she describes the experience in dramatic detail. "You could feel the way Mrs. Teichman was just looking right through you," she says with an exaggerated shudder. "Like she knew *exactly* what you were thinking."

"Ugh," Tammy says, and she does another cartwheel, nearly crashing into Ariella. "I feel like I'm going to sit there and confess to all of it. I didn't do it!" she adds hastily. "But I get so *nervous*."

"You were really quick," Meira observes to Gayil. "I guess I was more of a suspect than you."

Devorah snorts. "Gayil? She'd *never*. If she were sneaking into school to pull practical jokes, it'd be, like, putting a little cupcake on every girl's desk." She pats Gayil's back. "Sugar and spice and everything nice, this girl. The best of the bunch."

Gayil says, "I would not. The frosting would get *everywhere*." She winks at Devorah, and I wonder at how easily she lies. It had always felt impressive, not sinister, until I had begun to think about why she might be doing it.

Sari is next, followed by Tzivia, and Noa after them. I watch them go to the back of the room, counting down the girls left until my turn with a sinking feeling. I'm not great at pretending, and I'm nowhere near the accomplished liar that Gayil is. Maybe there's no proof, but I have no idea what I'll say when I'm questioned. Maybe I'll crack and admit it all. Maybe I'll look so suspicious that Morah Neuman will know right away.

Tammy does another cartwheel, and Gayil says from where she's sitting with Rena and Devorah next to the wall of the stage, "Tammy, you're giving me a headache. Can you cut it out?"

"Sorry." Tammy bounces on her feet, her hands moving aimlessly, and I feel sorry for her. She looks terrified.

Gayil must feel bad too, because she says, "You can *do* them. Just not where everyone's standing. Go up onto the stage."

I hear it only absently, fixed on the corner of the room where Rena is being questioned right now. She keeps touching her hair, a nervous gesture that cements her as an innocent in this, and Mrs. Teichman dismisses her quickly. She calls, "Shaindy Goodman?" and it's my turn.

My heart is in my throat. I can feel my heartbeat pulsing in my ears like a constant hoofbeat, making my whole body vibrate against my skin. When I walk, my feet are slow, and lifting them feels like raising giant weights and letting them fall to the ground. And there is something else, something I can't quite put my finger on . . .

Morah Neuman says again, "Shaindy?"

I look at her. I turn back to look at Gayil, who is chatting with Rena with a bored look on her face. And then I realize exactly what's about to happen, and I run.

CHAPTER 16

Tammy is poised at the top step of the stage, hands outstretched to begin her cartwheel. I barrel to the stage stairs, a shot of sheer adrenaline making me move faster, cry out louder. "*Wait!*"

Tammy turns, looking bewildered, and the rest of the class stares at me. "Shaindy?" Tzivia says. "What's wrong?"

I gesture breathlessly at the stage, and I have nothing to say that makes sense—nothing that is honest. "It looks like they mopped up here," I say, struggling to catch my breath. "Tammy, you're going to slip—" She might have fallen off the stairs or worse, and it would have all been because of me.

The teachers have made their way across the room, and Morah Neuman is tall enough to reach the stage floor easily. She swipes a finger across it, and she says, her brow creasing, "This isn't soap. There's something . . ." She moves her finger to her nose and sniffs it. "Is this *bubble bath?*" she says.

"Another practical joke," Mrs. Teichman says grimly. "This one could have severely injured a student if not for your quick thinking." She turns the force of her stern face on me, and I shudder, sure that I've implicated myself. But she smiles instead, and warmth quiets the adrenaline in my system. "Well done, Miss Goodman."

Tammy backs down the steps, and the other girls move to give the stage a wide berth. "That was a close one," she says, looking shaken. "I didn't even notice that the stage was wet. I just figured it was clean." She puts a hand on my arm. "Thanks, Shaindy. Pretty sure you just saved my life. Or at least my arms and legs."

A few other girls chime in—they'd noticed the shine to it, they hadn't thought about it, and they're all impressed with *me*. There are more hands on my back and arms, more smiles at me than I've ever seen before, and I am not invisible anymore. For a brief moment, I'm a hero, and it feels like something I can get used to. Like something I never want to lose again.

Mrs. Teichman clasps her hands together. "We'll put the questions on hold," she says. "I'm going to call a custodian to come and take care of the mess on the stage, but I don't want anyone in this auditorium right now. Please pack up and go back to your classroom. You can work on your Succos projects during the extra time you have until the davening period is over." She spares another smile for me, and I smile back.

It falters as we start to pack up, everyone chattering about what had just happened. I'm a hero, but I'd also helped Gayil put out the bubble bath in the first place. I'd been the one who'd created this mess, and now I'm . . .

We couldn't have anticipated this, I remind myself. We'd done it for the effect of the bubbles, and we hadn't known that Tammy would do cartwheels on the stage—

Except Gayil had been the one to suggest it, hadn't she? I stop short, my hand on my backpack zipper. Gayil had sent Tammy up there. But she wouldn't have tried to *hurt* Tammy. She couldn't have.

How would she have planned any of this? It's too elaborate. She'd have had to know that Tammy would be doing nonstop cartwheels, that she'd have needed a place.

But of course she'd need a place. We were here last night. The benches had already been out then. And we both know that Tammy does cartwheels when she's nervous, because we'd both been on her team for color war in camp, when she'd told us that—

And then, in a clear and horrible instant, the pieces all come together. Five days. Five pranks. Five potential targets. And none of those girls have anything in common, are in similar groups of friends, or live in the same development or are at the same place academically. There are no clear connections between them.

There hadn't been any clear connections between us when we'd all been in camp together either.

Rena's hair. Sheva's notebook. Sari's bee allergy. Tzivia's test. And Tammy's cartwheel. The five girls from our class who we'd shared a bunk with this summer. Gayil *has* been targeting them, sabotaging them each in underhanded ways. Why? What is she trying to do? And if she's gone after every other bunkmate in our class, then why hasn't she done anything to me? What is the point of all of this? How do I fit in?

I twist around and walk to Gayil, ignoring our agreement to keep our friendship hidden in school. "I need to talk to you," I say in a low voice, as Rena looks on curiously. "Now."

Gayil looks bewildered. "Uh, okay?" she says. She's a better actress than I've ever imagined, so good that I'm embarrassed by her tone.

I look down, catch sight of her charm bracelet, and see that she isn't wearing my *S* today. Instead, there's a little music note hanging from it, wound around a pretty *A*, Gayil's favorite charm. It feels like an ominous change. "Alone," I say, glancing at Rena.

Gayil gives me an awkward, vague smile. "Later, okay? We kind of have to go to class?" she says, jabbing her thumb at the double doors to the auditorium. I hang back, chastised and humiliated and so confused, and I hear her murmur, "*Weird*," to Rena as they file out of the auditorium.

Something is wrong. Something is *so* wrong, and I don't know what. I thought I knew Gayil, but I don't understand her at all. I thought that I understood her motivations, but I have even more questions now than I did before. Why? How? And why not me?

We go up the stairs slowly, Tammy hanging on to the railing as though she's afraid her feet might still slide out from under her. I shift around her to get upstairs a little faster, my heart racing and my uncertainty blending with fear. Maybe I'm wrong. Not about Gayil's targets, but about it all. She'd brought me along with her for a reason, and I'm less and less certain that it's because she'd liked me or seen me as a good ally. Why would she? She'd barely given me the time of day in camp. Even when everyone had played my game—

When Gayil had *disappeared*, and we'd thought it was nothing, and I'd—

A chill runs down my spine, a shiver of guilt in my panicked unease. Why have I been spared? *Have* I been spared?

I'm the first into the classroom, the others just behind me, and I push the door open and take two steps into the room before I freeze.

Everything is as we'd left it yesterday, our desks clear and organized in straight rows across the room. Everything, except for a pile of Succos projects flung across the desk, the velvet fabric torn from the boards and sequins and pins everywhere. "Oh, no," Temima whispers from behind me, sniffling.

Morah Neuman is at the door, and she moves past us swiftly, staring at the projects in consternation. "Not all of yours," she says, her commanding voice at once reassuring. "There are just a few on this pile."

We press forward around her as she lifts each board, finding the name on the other side. With a sick feeling in my stomach, I know exactly whose names they'll be. There are six of them, and the pins and sequins are everywhere. "Sari Klien," Morah Neuman reads. "Sheva Cohen. Tzivia Krasner. Rena Pollack. Tammy Seidenbaum." She lifts the last on the pile, and I know immediately whose name is going to be underneath it, and exactly how this is going to go. I know that I haven't been spared at all, and that this has always been about me, more than any of the other girls. "Gayil Itzhaki," Morah Neuman reads, and then, in a very different voice, "Wait."

There is something glinting beneath the mess of the final board, a broken little silver piece of jewelry. I close my eyes. Morah Neuman says, "Whose charm is this?"

"That's Shaindy's," Sari says. "I remember it from camp. Shaindy had that S charm. I got one too, but mine is gold." I open my eyes to see her hold up her wrist, displaying her own charm bracelet. The apple charm hangs mockingly from mine when I lift it, and a few girls step away from me.

Morah Neuman says, "Sari, please go ask Mrs. Teichman to come here."

For the second time today, all eyes are on me. But now, they don't look friendly or impressed. Instead, there is distrust on their faces, and I have nothing to say to defend myself. I look suddenly, desperately, to Gayil, but what can I do? This prank makes it clear that Gayil is a target too. No one will believe me over her right now.

In a clipped voice, Morah Neuman says, "Shaindy, with me." I follow her out of the classroom, trembling. My classmates move to the side, parting to create a hallway for me to the door, their accusing eyes boring into me. I want to deny it. I want to protest. I want to point a finger at Gayil, who is watching me with cold, cold eyes.

I am afraid of her, I realize suddenly. I am the only one here who knows what Gayil is capable of, and I am *terrified*. Morah Neuman opens my locker, and I see what she will, what I haven't noticed before in the chaos at the bottom of the locker. There's a notebook tucked in near the bottom, sandwiched between two old booklets, and Morah Neuman moves them aside and takes out the notebook. It says, **SHEVA COHEN: DO NOT TOUCH!** in bold letters across the front, and I am suddenly dizzy.

Morah Neuman turns back to the door, and I want to sob, to stop her from opening the door and showing this new, impossible evidence to the rest of the class. But I can only stand there as she eases the door open and stands against it, holding up the notebook.

Sheva rushes forward and seizes it, glaring at me where I stand in the hallway opposite the door. I can see Gayil near the teacher's desk, watching me impassively, her friends beside her.

Rena says, "I found a pencil in my locker. It was *covered* in slime. I didn't know whose it was because it was a Camp Kinor pencil, but Shaindy went there too. All seven of us did." She casts a look at me, touching her hair again, and I shudder at the poison I can see in her expression.

Morah Neuman holds up a hand. "Girls, sit down," she says, this time colder, and she lets the door close again, leaving me alone in the hallway with her. She stalks to my locker and pulls out my pencil holder. It's a pink mesh metal cup, a magnet on one side so it'll stick to the inside of locker, and there are a few pens and pencils in it, including a second Camp Kinor one. And at the bottom of the cup is a small, plastic rectangle, one that we both recognize instantly.

The key fob, sitting in my locker, the final piece of evidence against me.

CHAPTER 17

I am so sorry." Ema keeps saying it, over and over, as though it might erase everything that I'm being accused of. She'd put on a wig to come to school even though she *never* wears hers except on Shabbos, and it's askew on her head, a little tangled at the ends as though she'd forgotten to brush it. In her haste to arrive, she must not have looked at a mirror, and there's a smudge of makeup under her eye. She looks just as disheveled as I feel. "I can't believe this. I don't know what's gotten into Shaindy."

I sit silently in the seat behind her, my hands on the smooth, cool plastic of the chair beneath me. Ema stands between me and Mrs. Teichman as though she can somehow protect me from the inevitable. The office is smaller than I remember, as though the gaily painted walls of it might compress around me if I sit here for too long. There are pictures on a bulletin board of various students over the years, all of their bright faces mocking me from the wall, and the desk in front of me is like an insurmountable mountain.

I haven't been able to speak at all since I'd been brought to the office, still shell-shocked and terrified of what might happen next. Ema clears her throat, the sound like a crackle of static in my ears. "She's a good girl. You can look at her elementary records. She's a good girl who tries hard and has never really succeeded socially.

Maybe this was . . . just an attempt to be noticed." She still looks chagrined. "I can promise you that there *will* be consequences. Shaindy isn't going to do something like this again, *ever*. If we can make sure that this doesn't go on her permanent record—you know how competitive high schools are here, and this is just the beginning of middle school—"

"I'm afraid we can't do that," Mrs. Teichman says firmly, and Ema sags. Mrs. Teichman looks apologetic, a sign of compassion from behind those sharp black eyes that have always frightened me, her square jaw softening. "I'm sorry, but this wasn't just an isolated incident. Shaindy has been sneaking into the school for a week and has stolen and damaged other students' property and put classmates into dangerous situations. Tammy Seidenfeld could have been badly injured today if Shaindy hadn't had a sudden change of heart."

I duck my head, miserable. Ema shakes her head. "It's not like her," she says again, and she turns to me desperately. "Shaindy, was this really you?"

I can't answer, just avert my eyes and feel tears threatening to fall. If I talk, I'll cry, and I can't cry right now. Ema turns back, defeated. "What punishment are we looking at?" she asks.

"I'm afraid it'll have to be suspension," Mrs. Teichman says firmly. "Wednesday until Friday, and she can return after Succos vacation. Shaindy will be expected to make up any tests or classwork that she misses, and she will be on probation for the rest of the year. Any other offenses will be grounds for immediate expulsion. And it will go on her permanent record."

Mrs. Teichman clears her throat. "There is one other matter," she says, and she presses a few keys on her computer. "We do have a recording of one of the incidents. Video didn't catch Shaindy, but there was audio—"

The nanny cam. Of course. She presses play, and I only hear faint whispers, frantic and quick. Ema's eyes widen. I don't understand, not until Mrs. Teichman focuses that laser glare at me again and says, "Who were you whispering to, Shaindy?"

I think about saying *Gayil* now, about telling Mrs. Teichman the whole story. But no one will believe me. Who would? What reason does Gayil have to attack girls in the class where she reigns?

I slump in my chair, and Mrs. Teichman purses the burgundy lips that match her jacket and says, "Well, then. I think it's time you went home."

Ema can hardly look at me as we walk out, her grip tight on my arm. "I don't understand," she keeps muttering under her breath. "I don't understand." Our white minivan is parked in front of the school, and I realize with sudden guilt that she's had to run out from work to prepare for this meeting and then come and get me.

We get into the car. I sit in the front seat, staring out the windshield, and Ema says in a tight voice, "Now would be a good time to explain."

I want to tell her about Gayil, about the strange and intoxicating sensation that had come with being her friend. I want to explain that I was just the sidekick, the girl who'd come along and not the mastermind behind it all. I want to make excuses, though there aren't excuses. Tammy could have gotten hurt today. Sari could have last week. Rena's hair is *gone*, probably for at least a year. And I'd been a part of it all. Gayil might have manipulated me, set me up, and betrayed me, but even explaining her role in this won't erase mine.

The words come out of my mouth, rough and unsteady. "I made a mistake," I say, and then we are home.

Ema casts me a pained look with that expression again— disappointment, but also the bewilderment that hurts me to acknowledge—and she says, "I've already missed an appointment this morning." Ema is an occupational therapist, and I know that she needs every job she can get. My heart sinks. "I need to get back to work. You're grounded. There will be no more nighttime adventures, because you aren't leaving the house for a month," she says, and then, her wide eyes turning gentle and imploring and her voice wobbly, "Shaindy, I want to understand."

But I can't say another word. I leave the car, unlock the front door, and go into my lonely, quiet house and lie down in bed. When I finally cry, it's in heaving sobs that wrack my whole body, like this misery is too much for me to contain inside my skin. I cry and cry until I'm so exhausted that I fall asleep, and I wake up only once the day is over and Bayla has just slammed the front door hard enough to make the whole house shake.

I can hear her downstairs, hear Ema's low voice as she fills Bayla in. Bayla sounds impressed. "Wow," she says, the words filtering up the steps. "I didn't think the school would ever dare suspend *Gayil Itzhaki*. How did that go over?"

Ema sounds bewildered. "What does Avigayil have to do with this?"

I hurry to the stairs quickly, before Bayla can say too much and create an even bigger mess, and I get there just in time to see Ema's eyes clear up. "Ah," she says. "They did say they thought that there was a second girl involved. This makes . . . a little more sense."

Bayla's eyes narrow as she looks up at me. "You're covering for Gayil?" she demands. "You know they'll scramble if they find out this was all her. No way they can suspend her, and they can't suspend you if she's just as guilty."

I shrug, suddenly very tired again. "It doesn't matter," I say dully.

"Of course it matters," Bayla says hotly. Her face is still flushed from the wind outside and the righteous anger on her face, and there is a strange admiration that I feel when I see her like this, as short and unremarkable as Ema and me but somehow brimming with energy like a fireball. Her voice is caustic, and it burns me even though I know that it isn't directed at me. "It's not right that you're getting all the blame when she was just as much a part of it. Let all her friends deal with the fact that Gayil is going after them." She moves to the phone, resting in its cradle on the bookcase by the door. "I'm going to call Shani Teichman and see if she can talk to her mother. This is ridiculous—"

"*Stop* it," I say. It emerges in something like a screech, sharp and terrified, and Bayla and Ema both stare at me in consternation. I shake my head, search for the words that I can't express. "They'd forgive Gayil. Do you get it? They wouldn't care, because Gayil is . . ." I can't explain the hold that Gayil has over the class, over the faculty, over everyone in school. Gayil would sail through this and endure with a few laughs and short memories. But if I expose Gayil—if I'm the one who tells them all what she's done—I'm going to suffer a lot more than a suspension. Gayil has the power to make me miserable for the next three years and beyond. "I just want to deal with this myself," I say, and Bayla's hand drops from the phone.

Ema frowns, torn, and she glances from Bayla to me to the window to next door. "Shaindy," she says, and there is less of the pain from before. She's still angry, but she understands me a little better right now, and that's a relief. I don't think I could handle the alienation I'm about to suffer in school *and* my parents' disappointment. By the time Abba gets home from where he teaches at a yeshiva, he'll get a more complete version of the story. "I would like to at least speak to Ilana Itzhaki about her daughter."

"No," I plead. "Please, just leave it to me. I'll be fine. I'll take care of it."

There is that tightness in Ema's face again, but this one I recognize. It's the same one that she gets whenever I admit that I'd been the last one without a group for a project, whenever a teacher has called over the years to note that I *struggle socially.* It's the look she gets when there's something she can't fix for me, and I used to be embarrassed by it. Today, it feels like a blanket around me, a quiet comfort of love that I haven't lost today. "There does have to be consequences for your actions," she says at last. "Whoever you were following, the things that you did were unacceptable. I'm putting away your Rollerblades for the time being."

"Okay," I say, biting my lip. I don't need them anymore. I'm never going to fit in with everyone else again, anyway.

But I remember for a moment—rollerblading with Gayil, her flushed face and grinning as she'd glided backward to catch me, the way she'd whooped when I'd gotten the hang of it. Rollerblading had been *fun* with Gayil, had become something I'd enjoyed instead of just something to learn to fit in. And rollerblading has become intrinsically tied to my not-quite-friendship with Gayil, has become part of that secret, twisted part of my life. My heart still leaps when I remember it, and the fall to the ground is that much harder.

My Rollerblades are still in school, sitting at the bottom of my locker with everything else I'd left behind. I won't be going back to get them, anyway.

Ema says, "I want you to know that . . ." Her voice trails off, and she looks out the window, watching someone approach with a dark glare that I've never seen on her before.

I move to follow her gaze. And there she is. Gayil must have taken her time getting home today, because she's back a little later than usual. She's chatting with Devorah and Rena in front of her house and mine, lingering on the sidewalk. She throws her head back and laughs at something that Devorah has said, and she looks free and happy and careless all at once, quintessentially Gayil.

All three of us watch her from the window, and I can feel the helplessness build up inside of me, the sense that Gayil is a force that we can never defeat. That this twelve-year-old girl is powerful enough that my mother can't do a thing against her, that my high school sister can't touch her, that our family will never be able to mar her family with the stain she's left on me. We are nothing compared to Gayil, and she is standing boldly in front of our house because she knows it.

Gayil waves to Rena and Devorah and wanders into her house. And I am suddenly filled with the determination that comes with someone who has nothing left to lose. I turn to Ema. "I know I'm grounded, but—"

"Go," Ema says, and she squeezes my hand and lets me walk out of the house, down the steps, and next door to the lion's den.

CHAPTER 18

Gayil's little brother looks confused when he opens the door. "Did our garbage cans fall over onto your lawn again?" Aharon asks, and he raises his voice. "Mommy—!"

"No," I say hastily. "I wanted to talk to Gayil. Is she home?"

I know that she is, but I still have to endure the wait, Aharon calling to Rikki, who runs upstairs to find Gayil and then finally returns with long brown hair swinging around her face to whisper into Aharon's ear. "She says to go upstairs," Aharon says, eyeing me curiously. "Her room is on the right."

I walk upstairs. Gayil's house is built exactly like mine, the staircase in the same place and the painted walls and finishing the only real difference. Fairview houses had been built with big families in mind, and the upstairs sports one master bedroom at the end of the hall and four more bedrooms crammed in around it. In my house, one of those rooms is a study and another is a guest room. In Gayil's house, every last corner of each room has a bed, bunk beds against every wall and beds against the bunk beds. There are ten kids in all, and the mess seems to fill the hallways, spilling out from various rooms as though it can't be contained.

It has always seemed like something to envy. Today, in the state I'm in, I'm overwhelmed by it, and I long for the clean, quiet halls of my house.

I know which room is Gayil's. It's opposite from the room that is mine in my house, the windows looking out at each other, and it feels suddenly like ages since I'd first seen Gayil in her window with that sign. A wild part of me wants to believe that this had all happened accidentally—that Gayil hadn't meant for me to be implicated, that this is all a misunderstanding, and that even if the rest of the class will hate me, I will still have Gayil.

But I know that it's wishful thinking from the moment that I see Gayil again, sitting cross-legged against her pillow with a book on her lap. There's a cross section of a shark swimming across the centerfold of it, and I've never thought that something was more apt.

Gayil doesn't look up from her book. "Close the door," she says, and I do. She sets the book down on her lap, her face grim, and she stares at me like she never has before. It is calculating, but there is no coldness in it. Instead, there's a heat that makes me recoil. "Shaindy Goodman," she says softly. "Shaindy, who has done so many terrible things, right before Yom Kippur. I told Morah Neuman, you know."

A strange, uncertain hope flares in my chest. "You did?"

Gayil watches me unsmilingly. "I told her about all the times you've tried to follow me at night. The way that you came over to me right after what almost happened to Tammy. The time that you nearly started something with me in the supermarket, while my little siblings were with me. I don't know what you had planned for me, but I was so *afraid*. I was your last target, wasn't I?"

I gape at her. "What are you talking about? Why are you pretending . . . ?" But I realize then exactly what she's saying. "You're covering yourself," I say faintly. "In case I say that you were with me. They'll just think it's my attack on you." Gayil has thought this through, has planned for everything. "It'll be my word against yours."

"No one is going to let you say a thing," Gayil says, staring at me. "No one will ever believe that I'd do any of the things that you did. I'm the girl they all hope their daughters will grow up to become." She curls her lip. "That's what our teacher said last year. I'm *perfect*."

It's strange how something so arrogant can be said with such disdain. But I can't deny it, no matter how much I might hate Gayil right now. "Yeah," I say. "You are. So I don't know why you feel the need to do this to me when you *know* how hard it is for me. What was the point? Did you think it was funny? Is this just some twisted joke?" I blink away the tears, threatening to return again. "You didn't even know I *existed* before last week."

Gayil doesn't move, the book still on her lap and her back still resting against her pillows. I'm standing, but I feel as though she towers above me, as though I'm cowering before someone I've wholly underestimated. "I knew," she says, and her voice is sharp and rough, rich with that hot emotion like rage and something else. "I haven't thought of anything else since that day in camp."

Now I'm confused. "What day in camp?" I dig back through my memories of our month in camp, of Gayil shining like she always does and the rest of us caught in her shadow. "You barely noticed I existed in camp." I had been in the back of her little posse, the seven of us a loose gaggle of mismatched girls who'd been united only by the school we'd had in common.

"I noticed," Gayil says scornfully. "I felt *bad* for you. I thought that it was a shame that you'd never really had friends, and I wanted to do something nice for you. Like a good Bais Yaakov girl." She spits that out with distaste, mocking like I've never heard her before. "So when we had that free day, I decided that you'd be my mitzvah. You suggested the game of hide-and-seek, and I said it sounded fun."

I remember that. It's one of my fondest memories from camp, the day when I'd suddenly been the leader, when I'd talked and everyone had listened. We'd played for hours, hiding around camp and finding each other, right up until Gayil had gotten sick of the game and disappeared to go do her own thing. "That's the terrible thing that I did?" I say, disbelieving. "I suggested a game you didn't like?"

Gayil scoffs. "I liked it just fine the first time we all hid," she says. "And the second time, I hid in a spot where I was sure that no one would find me, near the ropes course." Had *that* been her big hiding place? I remember that we'd checked there, even though we'd all been nervous about it. The ropes course is on the far side of camp, through a little path into the woods, and it's a creepy place even during the day. Sari had been the one searching that round, and she'd dragged the rest of us there only once she'd found us.

"We looked there," I say, though I have no idea what we're talking about anymore. How is any of this about what Gayil had done to me? "You weren't there."

And something crosses Gayil's face, raw with pain like I've never seen before. "I got lost," she says, and I stare at her, bewildered. "I went in too deep and got turned around and got lost, and then I was in the woods, alone, and no one came to find me. I was so *sure* someone would come," she says, her voice haunted. "I was so sure that you'd call for help. But no one came."

"But you were back in the morning," I say slowly. I remember it, Gayil laughing in the morning as though she'd never disappeared the day before, teasing Rena and shrugging it off like we hadn't been worried or confused. I'd been a little annoyed too. To me, it had just been Gayil snatching the limelight again, finding a reason to draw attention to herself when I had finally gotten a tiny little spark of light of my own. "We went around when we couldn't find you. We called for you and said we'd given up. We thought you were just—"

"I was *terrified*," Gayil says, and that fury is back in her voice, barely contained. "I spent the night shivering in the woods, surrounded by animals that could have bitten or stung or *eaten* me—I wandered around until morning. I got *this*," she says, and she pulls down her knee sock to show me an old scrape, long and jagged, that's been picked at just enough that it hasn't healed. "I've never been so alone and afraid in my life. And then, finally, just after sunrise, I found my way back to camp. I thought there'd be search parties. I thought *someone* would have been looking for me. And do you know what Rena told me in the morning, when she complained that I'd *gone without her*?"

She raises those eyes to me, hot like coals. "She said that some of you were worried. That Tzivia had wanted to tell the counselors that I was missing. And that you—*you*, who I'd decided to be *nice* to, who I'd thought needed my *mitzvah*—you told everyone not to bother. That it was just *Gayil being Gayil*, whatever *that* means, and that I'd be back when I felt like it." Her voice is low but strident, vicious and lost all at once. "I was scared and alone, and you did everything you could to keep me in those woods. You told my friends to *cover for me*. Tammy and Rena put a pillow under my blanket at curfew just so no one would know that I was gone! And I was hiding from bears in the woods, trying not to breathe so they wouldn't hear me."

Her eyes are haunted now, brimming with terror and grief for some part of herself that she'd lost in the woods. I am silent for a moment, lost in that magical day that had been *mine*, that had been perfect and had made the entire camp experience worth it. My dream had been Gayil's nightmare. She'd had a cold the day after, had been sick and lethargic, and had begged to be excused from any activities, and I hadn't thought anything of it. "We made a mistake," I say at last. "But no one knew. How were we supposed to know?"

"Oh, *please*," Gayil snaps. "Don't pretend that you were an innocent in this. I know exactly why you did it. I know *you*, Shaindy. I know you perfectly. And I know that you were just so *happy* to be the center of attention, to be the one who everyone listened to, that you threw me away without a second thought. Don't tell me you didn't secretly wish that I'd *never* come back. You're pathetic, you know? A desperate outcast who will *never* be me, no matter how hard you try to eclipse me. And now you'll never have a friend again." She clenches her fists. "I've made sure of that. I want you to be scared like I was, to know what it feels like to be so *helpless*."

She laughs suddenly, bitter and harsh, and leans her head back against the wall. "I know," she says. "It's not what a Bais Yaakov girl would do. Tell me the truth, Shaindy. Aren't you tired of it? Of all of us with our perfect middos, flawless little girls all stacked up for everyone else's approval? Aren't you tired of being *sweet?*"

I can feel it, the exhaustion that is deep-seated now. It's been a lifetime of it. *This is how we react. This is what is appropriate. Rise above, be an example to everyone around you.* I am in the shadows, still trying to do what's right. Gayil has been performing every day of her life. "I don't think you were ever sweet," I say honestly, because now I understand Gayil like no one else in the universe does.

Gayil smiles a fierce, furious smile. "No," she says. "And now I'm very, very angry."

She laughs again. "I know why you did it," she says. "You can say it was a mistake, but we both know. Deep down, you wanted me gone. I know you too. You think that you like me—that you want to be me—but really, you hate me because I have what you want." She gets up, stalks toward me, and I am afraid again, terrified of this seething rage that seems to propel Gayil now.

I don't move. There is something else rising beneath the fear, a flowing energy that slams into Gayil's rage and holds it at bay. *Anger,* my own, and it surges through me to bolster me. I am furious at Gayil, and not only for the suspension or for the way she'd set me up. I am furious at the *lies,* at the week she'd spent building up the friendship I'd always wanted. It surges through me, erases every last bit of sympathy that I had felt toward her, and it makes me stronger than I've ever felt before. "I don't want any of what you have,"

I snap, and I really believe it for an instant. "But I can take it from you. I can prove that you were the one behind the pranks."

Gayil scoffs. "The principal will never believe you," she says.

"Maybe not," I concede, and it all seems so *simple*, suddenly, when I put aside all the parts of me that want desperately to be a good person. To be the girl that my teachers and family and the whole world seems to think that I am. "But you know who will?" And I remember what I've studied, the careful dynamics between Gayil and the others, the lingering question of a locker combination. "Rena Pollack will," I say triumphantly, and Gayil looks sharply at me. "She knows you're angry at her. And she was there in camp that day. Let's see if she thinks that some scratch on your leg is worth her hair." I can feel it, the power surging through me, the capacity that I have to *hurt* without consequence. It's something so potent that I can get lost in it, that I grasp how Gayil could do so many terrible things because of it. "Let's see what Devorah thinks, once Rena knows the truth. Let's see what the teachers believe then."

Gayil's eyes darken. "Let's see," she says, and I turn from her room and stride downstairs, my fury like a wave carrying me out to sea.

CHAPTER 19

The first thing that I need to do is gather evidence. But the evidence is scarce. Gayil has been careful, and the traces of her involvement are all subjective. There is a missing bee trap in her Succah, replaced by a brand new one, but that means nothing. Would her mother notice missing bubble bath? Would she do anything about it, or just shrug it off? Tzivia's crumpled old test might still be in her sweatshirt; but even if I can get it somehow, no one will believe that I didn't put it in there.

The only proof I have is the apple charm, hanging from my wrist, but even that is shaky evidence. Gayil hadn't worn it to school before, had never been seen with it, so why would anyone think that it wasn't just mine? Only my mother and Bayla believe me, and it'll be their word against Gayil's. I can imagine the conversation already, Mrs. Teichman saying, *I'm sure you want to believe the best of your daughter, but she does seem to have it in for Avigayil.* Ema won't be a reliable witness for me. There might be some doubt, but not enough to implicate the daughter of a member of the board and one of the shining stars of Fairview Bais Yaakov.

I *hate* her. I didn't before. She's wrong about that. But I despise her now like I've never hated anyone, like an obsession that I can't shake. I lie in bed that night and think about her falling in the bubble bath instead and hurting her leg, of her being the one exposed as the prankster and watching all the admiration directed at her turn to disgust. I want to see her *cry*. I want to see her as miserable as I am.

Overnight, the weather seems to change to suit my mood. The mild summer winds intensify into full-blown gales, hurling fire-orange leaves from the young trees of the development, and I sit outside in the cold without a coat, exulting in the chill of the wind on my face.

There is a creaking noise behind me and I turn around in time to see the door sliding open, and then Ema's hurried foot-falls thumping in my ears. She holds my coat tightly against her, but I don't take it, only watch the leaves flying down the street as though they're being pursued. The wind slaps against my face, and I luxuriate in the sensation instead of turning away from it.

Ema looks at me with tired, sad concern, the pity and grief that she always seems to feel when I'm upset. "Are you sure you want to be out here this early?" she asks, lingering on the porch. The first few kids are already leaving their houses, backpacks slung over their shoulders and older siblings calling after them with sweatshirts and coats.

I nod, and Ema goes back inside. Bayla wanders out of the house a few minutes later, picking up a friend across the street and waving to me as she heads out toward her high school. I watch the bus stop across the street, where elementary-aged boys all cluster together, each of them in a white polo shirt and black pants. There are a few similar clusters along the block, groups of boys and girls dressed in grey and white and blue uniforms, the wind whipping leaves around their legs as they await their buses.

The kids who go to school down the block emerge later from their identical, pink-and-white sided houses. They walk slower, wandering freely through the development, and the buses that arrive inch forward behind them. I watch as two of the younger Itzhakis leave their house together, chins in their coats and matching backpacks hanging from their hands as they walk. Gayil has the same backpack, and I vaguely remember what she's said about hand-me-downs in her family.

I brush it aside and watch, instead, the far side of the development, where Rena and Devorah live. *Far* is subjective here, just another block and a half away, but it does mean that Gayil is the last stop in the morning. I have watched them do this a hundred times, and I know exactly when they will arrive. They're all very punctual.

At 8:22 a.m. on the dot, Rena appears at the corner, gliding down the street in front of a patient bus. She has a hat on, though there is no mass of black curls beneath it anymore. Behind her is long-legged and freckly Devorah, who moves to the sidewalk first, and Rena follows a moment later. Devorah spots me on my porch first, and she slows down to nudge Rena and nod toward me. I wave at them, and I can feel the confidence running through me now. It makes me sit up straighter, makes my smile more edged, and Rena stares hard at me.

"Hi, Rena," I call to her. Rena stares at me, her hand going to her hair and her eyes flashing.

"Don't talk to me," she grits out.

Devorah puts a hand on her shoulder. Warning, always warning, because we don't get to be angry. It's not our way. It's not what's right.

Nothing is right anymore. "It wasn't my idea," I say, loud enough that they can hear me. "I just watched it happen."

Rena stops short, her heels slowing the wheels beneath her feet. "What do you mean?" she says. "You watched—?"

It's in that moment that Gayil flies from her house, her coat flapping behind her and her face more harried than I've ever seen it. "Let's go," she says swiftly, and she casts me an anxious look that might be genuine or might be put on. "Don't *talk* to her, Rena, you know she has it in for us."

Rena bobs her head. "You don't need to remind me," she says, shuddering, and she moves along with Gayil, out of earshot of me.

That's fine. I hadn't been planning on telling Rena anything yet. Two can play at this game. Gayil wants me to be afraid of losing everything? Well, she can be afraid too. It's spiteful and cruel and vicious, everything I've always been told never to do, and it's exactly what I've learned from her. I *am* Gayil now, just not in any of the ways that I'd thought I would want to be her. I am everything that would appall the model class where I've been for eight years.

I wonder if other girls feel this way too. If they know what kind of liquid power flows through our veins when we let ourselves forget about the consequences and the eyes on us. I might be at home, suspended, an outcast more than I've ever thought was possible, but I'm not done yet. I won't be done for a long, long time.

I think suddenly of Gayil in those woods, alone and afraid and furious, and I refuse to let myself feel guilty. I hadn't been the one to tell her to hide in such a *stupid* place. Doesn't she know better than to get lost in the woods? Hadn't the camp reminded us, over and over again, that the woods are off-limits? But Avigayil Itzhaki, who had never experienced a situation where she hadn't excelled, had never thought that something bad could happen to her.

What a *joke*. How bad could one night, spent alone and forgotten, be? I've spent a lifetime like that, and I'm fine. Better than fine. I don't have to worry about losing friends now when the only one I'd ever had had been a lie. I don't have to worry about the teachers being disappointed in me because they'd never really had any expectations of me. Gayil's night in the woods is my everyday, and I'm about to make it hers too.

When Ema leaves for the day, it's with a gentle warning. "I want you to review what you've been learning in school so you don't fall behind," she says. "I'll pick up your textbooks and sefarim on my way home and email your teachers today to get an idea of what you'll need to do."

And then I'm alone. Outside, the streets are still full—our development is never quiet. Now it's all toddlers and mothers, a few playgroups at the park across the street with a nursery full of children. Inside though, the house is still, and Gayil's house beside mine is, as well.

I daven, though my heart isn't in my prayers, reciting familiar words and letting my mind wander as I do. I'm still planning furious plans that I know will never come to fruition. Today, I'll break into Gayil's house and find some evidence of what she'd done. I know that their patio door is constantly left unlocked because I've heard Gayil's mother reprove the kids about it. Today, I'll show up outside school and stare at my classmates at recess, telling them everything that Gayil has done. Today, I'll come up with a prank of my own, and somehow sabotage Gayil.

123
• • •

But none of these are enough. None of these will do enough to persuade anyone that Gayil is the guiltier one, only make it clear that I have some vendetta against her. I have to be clear, and I have to tell someone the whole story and make sure that they'll listen. No one will let me speak for long enough to be convincing, not when it's about Gayil.

I take a fantasy novel off my shelf, one of Bayla's that I haven't read before, and I settle down onto Bayla's bottom bunk. I read the first page, then the second, then go back to the first when I realize that I'm not paying attention. I turn pages, make it all the way to the second chapter, and then notice that I haven't read a word.

I move to the desk to see if I can focus there. The window at the desk looks out at the backyard, and I can see the construction site over the fence, workers shouting to each other and large, lumbering machines moving through it. They swing big blocks of concrete from side to side, clanging and drilling in a cacophony of what looks like chaos to me. The sky is overcast above the trucks, and the noise is like a hammer pounding against my head, defying my quest to be distracted. I set the book down, and I open the drawer where Bayla keeps a plastic-wrapped stack of lined paper. And then I write.

My pencil scrapes against the paper as loudly as the screech of metal on metal outside. I start with the beginning, Gayil at her window with that sign, and I painstakingly describe every incident that had followed. The slime, and how Gayil had insisted that Rena would know right away. The notebooks. I hadn't known that Gayil would take Sheva's, or that it would be in my locker. I don't think it *had* been in my locker at all until yesterday. I write that too. I make bullet points and then squeeze in other things as I remember, organizing and reorganizing it all until everything is there.

Here is what I take responsibility for: Rena's hair. The bees. The bubble bath. The rest is all Gayil, and the parts of this that are my fault are much less egregious than the ones that are Gayil's. I remember to exaggerate some parts—how Gayil had known that Sari was allergic to bee stings and had meant for her to be hurt, because she *must have*. How she'd told Tammy to go on the stage to do her cartwheels. How Gayil hadn't just been working on harmless pranks, but is dangerous. I rewrite the whole thing neatly on paper, filling three pages with my retelling of the pranks, and then I sit back, satisfied.

I don't realize that I've spent the entire day on it until I hear the front door slam and Bayla come running up the steps, jogging into our room. "Wow," she says, smirking at me. "You really spent the whole day working? I would have napped."

"I was writing," I say, and I hold up the final draft. "No one will keep listening if I mention Gayil's name. But here, it's already written." I have plans. "I'm going to use the printer to copy the pages, and then send one each to Dr. Itzhaki, Mrs. Teichman, Morah Neuman, and Rena and Devorah. Let them all see what a *monster* Gayil is." I lean forward in my seat, full of too much unused energy from the past few hours, the anger like a sugar rush that won't fade. "She's dangerous, you know. I bet she would have been happy to see Sari stung or Tammy fall. She shouldn't be suspended. She should be *expelled*. And I'm going to be the one to take her down."

Bayla's brow furrows, her bag dropping to the floor next to the doorway. "Whoa," she says. "Are you sure you're Shaindy?"

"I'm new and improved," I say, and I feel it, the ripple of fury that accompanies every word. I am changed, and I move differently, speak with a harsher cadence. "I'm not ready to give up. If I'm going down, I'm going to take Gayil with me. Let her get a taste of what it's like to be me." I feel it, the smug righteousness that comes with fighting back. It feels *good*.

Bayla sits on her bed, still watching me with a strange wariness on her face. "Look," she says. "I thought about it. And I think it's okay to name Gayil as the leader in all of this. But this is..." She flips through the papers. "Shaindy, you're so *angry*. I haven't seen you this angry since that time I broke your favorite toy, and you were *four*."

I shrug. "I have the right to be angry." It still courses through me, an adrenaline that is beginning to feel exhausting. I can't let go of it. I can't stop.

"Yeah," Bayla says, and she lies back on her bed, tugging off each of her thick knee-high socks with the toes of the other foot. "Sixth grade is a *rough* year. And this is rougher than most kids will get. But this isn't going to make you any friends. It's just going to make people afraid of you." She sighs. "Not to sound like a teacher, but Yom Kippur is in five days. It always feels like that day for me, you know? The one when you really can start over new. This isn't going to be a fresh start. It's going to be a bloodbath."

"Good," I say, defiant. "It's exactly what Gayil deserves. I thought you were on my side."

"I am," Bayla says, but she still stares at me, troubled, until I'm uncomfortable and stomp out of the room to make my photocopies.

CHAPTER 20

I fold the copies and place them in envelopes, and then I make another one, this one for Gayil. I write her name on the envelope in clear letters, and then I go over to her house and give it to the sister who opens the door. She looks at it dubiously, and then says, "Gayil says I'm not supposed to let you come upstairs. She says you're *crazy*."

My jaw ticks. I say, "She'll want to see this."

And then I go back home. I wander into the kitchen. Abba is making dinner tonight, putting together a concoction that looks like mashed potatoes with everything else in the freezer inside of them. He has a little white smear of mashed potato on his auburn beard, and he's digging around in the fridge, the bottom of his tzitzit strings stuck in the vegetable drawer. He pops his head out of the fridge and says, "Shaindy, what do you think about pickles?"

"In the mashed potatoes?" I ask dubiously, scrunching up my nose, and he laughs and pulls the jar out of the fridge anyway.

"Your mother has something for you in the living room," he says, dicing a pickle, and I wrinkle my nose and head into the living room.

Ema is sitting there, a box on her lap, and she looks uncertain. "I don't know if this is a good idea or not," she says, and she taps her fingers against the box. "It feels a little like I'm rewarding bad behavior. But I did make you a promise, and I see that this is . . . well, you're going through something very difficult right now." She takes a breath. "And I know that it's only going to get harder. So I'm rescinding my original punishment."

"You're giving back my Rollerblades?" I say. She must have taken them from my locker, then, and giving them back is supposed to be a gift. But I can't think about wearing them right now, not when they're one of my best memories with Gayil—

But Ema opens the box, and it isn't Rollerblades at all. It's a brand-new pair of Heelys, the ones I'd been begging to have for weeks, purple and blue with the word *HEELYS* displayed across them. They aren't even a knock-off brand, and I unconsciously start doing the math, figuring out exactly how much they must have cost. "Wow," I manage to say, and I take a step forward, feeling abruptly as though I want to cry again. "They're really . . ."

Ema holds up a hand. "Everything you did was wrong," she says. "Unacceptable, no matter who the ringleader was." Her face softens. "But I think that you'll stand out enough in school right now, and if this makes it easier to go back . . ."

I move to her, hugging her tightly, the Heelys dropping to the floor, and then I lace them on in a hurry and sail through the house. I'm not brave enough to go outside right now, even to try out the Heelys, but there is something so wonderful about them— about this thing that is all mine, that I'm *good* at—and I keep them on even when I clomp upstairs after dinner, my stomach still debating if pickles and mashed potatoes are a good combination.

I glance out the window as I enter the room, absentminded, and then I stop. Gayil is framed in her own window, staring across our yards at me as though she's been waiting for me to return. I glare at her, and Gayil glowers back, the two of us frozen in fury. I can see my letter clutched in her hand, and I know that she finally believes that I can ruin her. *Good.*

And then, she raises a paper in her other hand, one word on it. *DON'T*, it says. I stare at her, disbelieving, and Gayil turns away. Her shoulders seem slighter today, the headband in her hair smaller and narrower than her usual, but her dark eyes still tear into me like claws. She takes a marker off the windowsill and writes quickly, her lips pressed together, and then lifts the paper again with another word on it. *PLEASE.*

Never have I held someone else's future in my hands like I do right now, knowing that even Gayil finds my accounting of the past week to be undeniable. I'm going to *win*, to take down the perfect girl, and I'm going to get the revenge that I deserve. Gayil is begging me, as though she has any right. As though this isn't all on *her*, and I've been her hapless victim.

I turn away deliberately, turning out my light, and Bayla says, "Hey," from the desk. "I was studying here."

"One second," I say, and I close the door too, until it's completely dark in my room and Gayil can't see in. Now I can watch her at the window, see the way that she sags and her face falls. It's a new expression on her, a defeat that I'd never imagine that Gayil could be capable of. It's *victory*, and it should feel . . .

It should feel . . .

"Shaindy!" Ema calls from downstairs. "You have a visitor!"

I flick the light on and leave the room, shooting one last glance at Gayil's window. She's gone, and I wonder with a rush of adrenaline if it's her, come to plead her case some more. Who else would be visiting?

But it's not Gayil. It's Tzivia at the door, and I feel the strangest sensation of relief at seeing her, settling the adrenaline in my stomach. "I didn't want to do it," I say right away. "I refused to do it. The test, I mean. I didn't want to hurt you—"

Tzivia waves an impatient hand as Ema looks on, Abba peering over from the kitchen, both of them very interested in what I have to say. "Forget that," she says. "Everyone is saying that someone helped you. It was Gayil, wasn't it?"

The trickle of relief becomes a wave, washing over me with Tzivia's certainty, and I nod sharply. "It was more like I helped her," I say, and, conscious of my parents' eyes on us, I add, "Do you want to talk upstairs?"

"Morah Neuman also talked to the class about you," Tzivia says, following me up the staircase. "She was really stern about it. Asked us which friends of yours might have been involved and the only person anyone suggested was me." She shakes her head, ponytail swinging against the collar of her navy polo, and I burn with humiliation by proxy, imagining a class where everyone knows that I don't belong. "Which says *plenty* about how nice our class really is. But Gayil . . ." She falls silent.

We go to the guest room, which is free of nosy sisters or neighbors staring in from the window, and we sit on one of the beds, cross-legged, as I tell Tzivia the story. I might have embellished some parts for the letter that will incriminate Gayil, but I don't have the courage to do that to Tzivia's face, when she had been one of Gayil's targets too. "But I'm going to take her down," I say swiftly. "And she knows it. I'm going to make sure *everyone* knows that it was her too."

"I don't get it," Tzivia says, stretching out her narrow legs across the bed. "I always thought that Gayil was . . . well, there was some-thing *off* about her. But why would she do all of this to you? To us?"

"For the *stupidest* reason," I say. It seems so silly to me now, Gayil's haunted eyes at something that had been perfectly fine in the end. "Remember that game of hide-and-seek in camp?" I tell her the story, explain where Gayil was, and how she'd blamed us all for what had happened.

To my surprise, Tzivia looks stricken. "Oh," she says, and she twists the dark blue comforter between her hands, tugging at it. "I always thought . . . well, you know what I thought about Gayil after that. I can't believe she was lost the whole time."

"She was fine," I say, dismissive.

"She got *lucky*." Tzivia shivers. "Remember when that boy went missing in the Catskills last year? That was . . . what, five hours? It felt like the whole Jewish world went out to find him, searching the woods. They said that if it got dark, they had no way of knowing if he'd ever be found. And Gayil spent the whole night out there." She looks thoughtful. "That changes a person, I bet."

"Don't tell me you feel bad for her," I say, and I laugh, because who would ever feel bad for Gayil, whose worst night ever was just a few hours in the dark in the woods?

But Tzivia's gentle eyes fill with grief. "I really thought that she was . . . hungry for attention," she says. "That she did it just because she wanted to mess with us. She could have died. She must have been so *scared*."

I'm beginning to feel uncomfortable. Tzivia is far more forgiving than I am. "Doesn't excuse what she did," I point out. "To Rena. To *me*."

Tzivia looks up at me, and she looks very uncertain. "I guess not," she says. "But she kept it a secret for so long. It must have really killed her. I wonder why she didn't just tell us what happened."

But this I know, with an uncomfortable awareness. When something so terrible happens that there's nothing that can make it right—whether it's out in the woods or being sabotaged by someone you trusted—the only way to keep going is to hold on to your anger. It's the only control we have. "She says that I did it on purpose," I say, and *this* I cling to, the unfairness of it all. "She decided that I hated her for being . . . well, *Gayil*, and she decided that I wanted bad things to happen to her."

Tzivia doesn't budge. "Well, didn't you?" She looks a little sheepish. "I know that I wouldn't have cried about it. Especially in camp. I was so lonely there," she says, and she bites her lip. "I went because my sisters loved it, but I didn't have friends in camp. I used to watch Gayil and be so *jealous* of her perfect life, the way that everyone immediately fell in love with her. I might have hated her a little bit for it." She worries the comforter a little more. "Maybe a part of me knew that it was the wrong thing not to tell anyone that she was missing. I don't know. But I didn't want her to be angry with me either." She sighs. "I don't know. It was stupid."

In the face of Tzivia's honesty, I feel a flicker of shame. *Had* I hated Gayil? Had I done what I did out of selfishness instead of ignorance? I search back through my memories, try to remember how I'd felt that day. When I'd been honest with myself, before I'd been angry, it had been the thing that I'd thought of when Morah Neuman had asked us what the worst thing we'd done had been. Because I *had* been delighted that everyone had listened to me that day. And when Gayil had disappeared, I had felt a nasty, ugly resentment toward her for stealing back everyone's attention. I'd encouraged everyone to stop looking for her because I hadn't been ready to cede the crown back to her. And when they'd agreed—when Rena had covered for Gayil and everyone else had laughed it off—I might have wondered, for a moment, if Gayil was all right. If I had, I'd swept it aside, because without Gayil there as a living reminder of our hierarchy, we were nearly all equals. I was nearly someone worth seeing.

I was Gayil's mitzvah that day, and I'd left her behind in the dust.

It feels like a chore to stay so angry right now, to maintain that kind of energy. It deflates in the face of Tzivia's honesty, and I set it aside and stare at Tzivia, who still looks so *sad* for Gayil. "You're a really good person," I say finally. "Not anything like me or Gayil."

Tzivia snorts. "That's fine," she says. "I don't think I could handle being Gayil. And I'd rather . . ." She looks at me, and I wonder why I'd ever thought that she was quiet. She isn't quiet at all. She chooses her words carefully, and she wields them in all the right ways, the real Bais Yaakov girl that I'll never be. "I'd rather be your friend than be you," she says, and it feels like the greatest gift that I could get right now.

"Really?" I say, and it's hard to believe that this friendship too, won't end in disaster. "After everything I've done to the class? After what I watched Gayil do to you?"

Tzivia shrugs. "Yom Kippur is coming, right?" she says. "It's a good time for forgiveness."

She climbs off the bed, tossing a glance back at me, and she says, "Whoa. Are those new Heelys?"

CHAPTER 21

Thursday. Day two of my suspension. The chill outside is beginning to seep into the house, where Ema hasn't made the call to turn on the heat yet. I put on a sweater and go through some of the schoolwork that Tzivia and Ema had brought me. It's easier than I remember to grasp the concepts in it, and I wonder if I might wind up doing well this year after all. Without anything else to fixate on, maybe I'll be able to pay attention and focus on schoolwork.

But after I've finished my schoolwork, there is little to do but think about what is yet to come. Yom Kippur is on Monday night, Succos next Friday night, and the school's Succos vacation begins tomorrow afternoon. I won't be back in school for another two and a half weeks, which should be plenty of time to hope that everyone will forget. It also means that I only have another day to tell them about Gayil before it'll get swallowed up by vacation, forgotten before it can ever get bad.

I remember Gayil in the window of her room, holding up that sign. **PLEASE.** There was no more of the teasing mystery on her face, no more mischief. She had looked like someone else entirely, afraid and defeated. I wonder if it's how she'd looked in the woods too, when she'd been all alone and had realized that no rescue would come for her.

It isn't *fair*. It isn't fair that she blames me for it, that I have to suffer because she did. It's a selfish, cruel thing that she's done—that she did to all six of us—and she deserves to be exposed. She deserves *worse*, but this is a start, and I look through my sealed, neatly labeled envelopes and contemplate bringing them to the school right now.

This is justice, when justice is left to us. This is what I have to do. What is *right* to do. I don't know why I have to convince anyone of that.

I don't know who I'm convincing right now.

I imagine Gayil in the woods again, and it seems laughable now, like something absurd that should have been a funny story. Since when does Gayil let a few hours in the dark keep her down?

Struck by an idea, I put on my Heelys and go outside. There are no forests nearby, but there is the construction site behind our development, loud and large and messy, and I walk around the blocks of our development and follow the sidewalk back to a poorly sealed fence. I slip through the fence, wander between large vehicles and pallets piled high with building material. I'm small enough that I remain unnoticed for a few minutes, and I sit in front of a pallet and hunch down, trying to experience that feeling that Gayil had felt when she'd been lost in an alien place.

The pallet is lifted without warning, and I stumble away, afraid I'll be yelled at. But the man operating the forklift that lifts it doesn't notice me, and I'm able to move behind a stationary crane—only for it to start moving too.

Suddenly, the whole construction site seems full of life, of movements and bangs and thumps, of things dropped around me and of trucks that could run right into me without seeing me. This had been a ridiculous idea, and I scamper away, trying desperately to get out.

I make it back through the fence, breathing thick and dirty air as I squeeze through the gap between green plywood walls and onto the sidewalk beyond it. I crouch down to press the button on the back of my Heelys that will pop the wheels out and push off one shoe to glide back home at top speed, my heart pounding from the experience. I've gained no deeper understanding of Gayil, nothing but dust stinging my eyes and a lump in my throat, and I sail past the curious eyes of nursery aides at the park and retreat into the house, frustrated and confused.

I kick off the Heelys, run upstairs, and scream into my pillow for a full minute, and then I collapse against it. Why do I *want* to understand Gayil? What is it about her that I just can't shake from my heart? Is it just that she's smart and popular and charismatic, this perfect girl living next door? Shouldn't the past weeks have cured me of this sickness?

I bury my face in my pillow and imagine Gayil in the woods again, that sagging, defeated expression on her face. I imagine the devastation this time, not the fear: the certainty that she is alone and forgotten, that no one is looking for her. I remember her sitting in my room, talking to me on Rosh Hashanah. *Nothing scares me more than being alone,* she'd said, and it had been a haunting, broken revelation, as broken as Gayil being positive that everyone hates her.

Maybe I'm just drawn to Gayil because, under the polish and shine, she is very much like me.

I read for an hour or so before I can't sit still anymore, and then I go downstairs and flip through the kids' cookbooks until I find something that we have all the ingredients to make. I spend another hour cooking dinner and washing the dishes, and then I clean the kitchen and dining room for Shabbos, tomorrow night.

By the time Ema gets home, the granite of the countertops is gleaming and the wooden table has been sprayed and wiped down. Four blue-trimmed dinner plates catch the light from where they're already laid out and a vegetable spaghetti dish is on the stove, and she looks startled and then very proud of me. "You're really growing up, Shaindy," she says, and she squeezes my shoulder as I grin at her. My life might be in shambles, but I don't think I'm done just yet. A switch within me has flicked, though I haven't fully figured it out.

I sit outside on the front porch while I wait for Bayla to get home, flipping through my math workbook to try to piece together what I'd missed in class. It's not much—we're still reviewing concepts from last year—but I hadn't been great at math last year either. This seems like a good time to catch up. I'm on a burst of productivity, and I don't want to lose it.

It's dismissal time and the end of the workday, and the streets are crowded with girls coming home from school and adults with strollers laden with their Thursday shopping for Shabbos. I refuse to let it bother me today. Instead, I write answers in my math book that look bumpy from the texture of the painted grey slats of the porch beneath it. I'm puzzling over the next problem when I sense that someone has stopped on the path up to my house. I look up, expecting a comment from Bayla about my sudden interest in math, but it isn't her.

It's Morah Neuman, watching me gravely, and all my new-found confidence fades away. I jump to my feet, and I glance nervously at the house next door. Gayil isn't home yet, but I can see, among the mass of uniformed girls returning from school, three figures moving on Heelys down the street. "Morah Neuman," I say quickly.

Morah Neuman inclines her head. "Shaindy," she says. "I wanted to check in and see how you were doing." Morah Neuman has been teaching at the school for *forever*, is old enough to have taught my mother, but she still carries herself tall and steady. I've never felt so intimidated by her as I do today, even when she sits on the porch steps and pats the spot beside her.

I sit. "I'm—I'm doing okay," I say, stammering a little. "Tzivia brought me the notes yesterday, so I've been keeping up with my studies—"

"I'm glad to hear that," Morah Neuman says. "And that Tzivia is visiting. I know that you two are close."

Close is an exaggeration of what's only barely a friendship, but I hear the leading note in Morah Neuman's voice, the suspicion that comes with it, and I say quickly, "We *aren't*. I mean, I *want* us to be, but she isn't—she wasn't the one who did the pranks. I promise." I bite my lip. "She's just *really* forgiving."

Morah Neuman sighs. "Shaindy," she says. "Is this really something you want to carry alone? I can't imagine that you were the instigator."

"Why not?" I ask, and I feel suddenly, unaccountably offended. "Because I'm not smart enough to pull off something like this on my own?"

"Of course not," Morah Neuman says hastily, shaking her head. "You strike me as a very bright girl who is . . . prone to distractions. But I just . . ." She sighs. "I just don't see you doing something so malicious to your classmates. And I worry about the person who did." I glance subtly at the house next door. Gayil and Rena and Devorah are all on the porch now, staring at us, and Gayil's lips are pressed together, her eyes fearful. Morah Neuman doesn't see me looking. "I worry what else she might do too."

The strength that runs through me now isn't that strong, powerful anger, but a new power, one that makes me nauseous when I imagine using it. I swallow. "She won't do anything else," I say at last, and I think that I'm right. "The fob she used was the one you found in my locker. It's how she—how *we* got in," I admit. "But I think it's done."

"Who—"

I gather all my courage, and I turn to face Morah Neuman, away from Gayil's worried face. "What's the point in telling you now?" I ask her. "It's over. It won't happen again. I know that. She did what she wanted to." Anger is so hard to maintain, to hold on to, and I am sure that it had all drained out of Gayil once she'd gotten her revenge. I can start the cycle again—can awaken it within her, can get my vindication, can watch as Gayil gets hers in return—but what is the point? What will we do, if not destroy everything in our wake?

There is a power too, in letting go. In taking the fury and refusing to let it control you. "She was angry," I say. "I know that isn't how we're supposed to be, but—"

Morah Neuman raises her eyebrows at me. "There's nothing wrong with being angry," she says in her dry voice. "Far be it from me to try to limit the emotional expression of sixth-grade adolescents." I stare at her, my heart unsteady as it pounds, and I am no longer proud or ashamed of my fury. It feels utterly ordinary, unremarkable, and I take a breath and leave it behind. Morah Neuman clears her throat. "But when that anger becomes poison—"

"If she does it again," I say, and this I mean. "If there's any sign that someone is hurting people in the class again, then I'll tell you who it was. I promise."

Morah Neuman contemplates this, and she looks at me with that suddenly piercing stare. "I hope that your friend appreciates what you're doing for her," she says carefully.

"Oh," I say, shrugging. "She's not my friend."

Morah Neuman leaves with another sharp look back at me, and I sit in silence, still uncertain about what I've decided to do. I don't get more than a minute to myself though. Gayil and her friends are piling toward me, the three of them discarding their grudges out of sheer curiosity.

"What did she say to you? She looked annoyed," Devorah says.

I shrug, looking directly at Devorah's freckled face and no one else's. "She wanted to know who I was working with. I didn't tell her," I add, and I still don't look at Gayil.

Rena sounds resentful. "So there *was* someone else. Well, at least tell *me* who it was. I was their *victim*."

I shrug again. "It's over," I say. "I'll leave it to them to decide when they want to tell you." *When*, I say, not *if*. Gayil will have to tell Rena someday if she wants to save that friendship. It isn't something that can stay secret forever. But my envelope, addressed in block letters to Rena Pollack, is not the way.

"Ugh," Rena says, and she scowls at me. "You really are terrible, aren't you?" I refuse to answer that. She turns to Devorah. "You know who I think it was?" she says. "I remember how Goldie *desperately* wanted to go to Camp Kinor. She probably hates us just for getting the chance."

Devorah laughs. "Don't be ridiculous," she says, and she rolls down the path away from me, Rena trailing after her. "Goldie can't keep a secret. She'd have told us it was her the day it first happened." They disappear down the street with a wave to Gayil, still floating theories loudly as they go.

Gayil stands still, exactly where she'd been. I haven't looked at her yet, but I know that she's there, and I wait for her to speak. "What do you want?" she says finally. "Are you going to blackmail me or something? Because I can still take you down. I *will*. I'll—"

"I don't want anything from you," I say, and it emerges gentler than I'd meant for it to. I clear my throat. "I'm sorry that we left you behind in the woods," I murmur, and I look up at Gayil. She is staring at me wide-eyed, unguarded again, and it keeps me talking. "I was selfish, and you were alone because of me."

Gayil is still staring at me. "I don't understand," she says, and she sounds frazzled, uncomfortable and anxious. "I don't know what you're trying to get from me—why you're saying all of this—why you didn't—"

"I wanted your forgiveness before Yom Kippur," I admit. It's been simmering for a full day, since Tzivia's visit. I can't put Gayil's pain out of my head, not even for my own. It feels strange, caring so much about someone who doesn't care about me. It feels right too. "I guess that's up to you. I won't tell either way. Come." I lead her inside, right in front of Bayla, who is coming up the walk now, and right past Ema, who stares at Gayil with marked distrust as she follows me up the stairs.

I find the envelopes on my desk, all five of them lying in a pile on my desk, and I tear them up in front of Gayil, shredding them into pieces. Gayil watches me, her face unreadable, and I watch her right back.

"Thank you," she whispers, and she shuts her eyes. "I'll tell Rena. I *will*. Someday, when I can. When it's not all so fresh."

"Okay," I say. "She's your best friend. She might understand why you were so angry." Or she might not, and we both know it. We might be the nicest class in the school, but we're far from perfect.

Gayil takes a breath. "I still don't understand," she says, and she watches me, her gaze steady and that darkness faded from her eyes. I am no longer afraid of her. And I find that her presence, once again, makes me bold instead.

"I still think we had something good together, even if it was all a lie," I say. It isn't an answer, but it is the only one I have. "I think that we . . . we understand each other in a way that no one else does. I know you now, better than Rena or Devorah or your sisters."

Gayil's voice is hoarse and raw, as though she might be close to breaking down. "I think so too," she says, and she jerks away from me as though she's been burned by the revelation, and she walks out of my room, leaving me alone.

CHAPTER 22

We get the call late that night, after I'm supposed to be in bed. I'm in pajamas but I'm downstairs, singing old songs with Abba as he polishes the silver candlesticks for Shabbos and I set the table, and Abba picks up when the house phone rings. "Rabbi Itzhaki," he says genially, twisting the earpiece of his tortoiseshell glasses between his fingers. "What can I do for you?"

I pause, clutching my stack of forks, and I watch as Abba nods, a barely audible voice on the other end of the phone. "I see," he says. "Well, we're very grateful. I'll let her know."

He hangs up the phone, and he looks very satisfied for a moment before he speaks. "Your suspension has been rescinded," he says. "You seem to have a friend on the school board who interceded for you." His eyes twinkle. "The principal has requested that you write an essay about your actions and hand it in after vacation, but you're welcome to return to school tomorrow morning."

I stare at him, uncomprehending. "What?"

Abba takes the forks from me. "Go to bed," he instructs me. "It's a school night!"

When I go upstairs, Gayil's light is off in her room, and I have no indication of what she's thinking. She'd spoken to her father—maybe even confessed it all to him, I don't know—and she'd fought for me to come back to school. Maybe this is how we're even now, how my kindness has warranted hers. Gayil can go on with a clear conscience, and I can too.

I crawl into bed, and I consider that, really, suspension might have been preferable to seeing my classmates tomorrow.

I'm even more sure of that in the morning, when I drag myself out of bed and pack my bag again. I'm wearing my new Heelys, a little less shiny after the trip to the construction site yesterday, and Ema has made me a special pancake breakfast before school. "I'm proud of you," she says.

I shrug. "I didn't *do* anything. I guess Gayil did."

Ema shakes her head. "You did *something*," she says. "It's hard to fight a battle like the one that you've been fighting for the past few days. But it's much harder to make peace."

"We'll still totally beat Gayil Itzhaki up for you though," Bayla chimes in, helping herself to some of my pancakes. I bat her away and she crosses her eyes at me and takes another one. "You know, if you want."

Ema tsks. "Yom Kippur!" she reminds Bayla, and she ushers us out the door to join the stream of kids heading to school.

Bayla walks with me today, picking up a few friends down the block before she leaves me behind. "Just be cool," she says. "Don't talk about it, and look confused at anyone who brings up what happened, like they don't know what they're talking about. I bet it'll blow over quickly." She says it with the confidence of someone with *friends*, and I file her advice away as good for someone else.

I see Tzivia across the street, and I dash forward and cross in front of a bus that honks at me to catch up to her. "Hi," I say breathlessly.

Tzivia looks startled. "I thought you were suspended."

"Not anymore. Someone on the board got involved," I say, and Tzivia's brow furrows. "I think it's going to be okay."

But it isn't exactly, not yet, and I get my first hint of that when Temima makes a beeline for Tzivia in our hallway and then stumbles back, casting me a dark look. Most of the class is already there, taking notebooks out of their lockers and putting their backpacks into them, and there are cool glances cast my way, distaste emanating from them at me. I try to keep my head high, making my way toward my locker.

Someone bangs into me, a little too hard to be accidental. Someone else giggles. Rena is already at her locker, and she stares at me with distinct displeasure. My locker is still a mess from when it had been inspected, and I shuffle my books back into it from my backpack, focusing on the back wall of it instead of the girls staring at me, unfriendly.

It's a relief to sit in the classroom, where Morah Neuman commands everyone's attention. "Your Succos projects should all be done now," she says. "Girls who had the . . . setback," she says delicately, her eyes sweeping around the room and passing right over me. "I have the plastics for yours here, so you can finish at home." She passes them out to Sheva, Rena, Tzivia, Tammy, and Sari. Gayil is the last to get hers, and she takes it unsmilingly. I try and fail to catch her eye. "Shaindy, I have one for you, as well."

It takes all my willpower to get up and walk across that room and take the plastic, my heart pounding in my chest and the eyes on me scorching. My head isn't nearly as high as it had been earlier, and I clutch the plastic tightly in my hand and go back to my seat. Morah Neuman says, "The plastic will make your boards waterproof for the Succah. The trick is to seal it around the board except for a little bit at the edge, then vacuum the air out of that opening before you seal it."

"Thanks, Morah Neuman," Gayil says, the de facto spokesperson for the class. I dare to pull my board out from under my desk. It's still in perfect condition, untouched by even my angry classmates. If nothing else, that speaks to how genuinely *nice* they are.

And I am no longer counted among their ranks. Shaindy who had been ignored is gone. In her place is Shaindy who is hated and feared, and I can feel the dread beginning to build within me again, the thoughts of doing this for the rest of the year. Morah Neuman says, "I like to do something special for my class on Yom Kippur. There is a shul in our auditorium where you can daven Neilah, the last prayer of Yom Kippur. Beforehand though, I want to meet in here with any girls who are feeling up to it. We'll talk a little about teshuva and Yom Kippur and try to gain the focus we'll need for Neilah."

She goes on, speaking a little about Yom Kippur before we daven, and I feel eyes on me. I glance to the side, and I spot Gayil looking quickly away before our eyes can meet.

Friday is a short day, so there isn't much time outside of the classroom. Even recess is indoors today, because it's drizzling outside. I stand alone during the break, listening to my classmates as they get ready for Yom Kippur with the same exchange as always. "I'm sorry for anything I did to you this year," Tammy says in a sing-song to Sheva. "Do you forgive me?"

"Do you forgive me?" Meira asks, three times rapid-fire at someone who won't answer, and she bounces with glee. "Ha! Three times. Now you have to forgive me."

"I'm sorry for anything I did, do you forgive me?" It's Rena, saying it to Gayil, and I watch out of the corner of my eye as Gayil laughs and nods. Gayil still sails through the classroom, untouched by any of what went so wrong for me this week, and it takes all I have not to resent her a little bit for it.

I'm not *perfect*. Instead, I am alone, but this time it's by design. No one comes over to me to apologize or ask for forgiveness. Glances are darted at me, almost expectant, as though I will go around and ask instead. But I won't subject myself to *that*, and I linger in a corner instead, eating a bag of chips and avoiding everyone's gaze.

There are whispered conversations that I know are about me, if only because everyone keeps staring. I slump against the wall, my confidence fading, and I stare at nothing instead.

Tzivia comes up beside me, her voice low, and she says, "Don't worry about it. By the time Succos is over, they'll all be over it." But she sounds doubtful, and she leans back against the wall and watches the room. "I heard that Morah Neuman's Yom Kippur class is the best thing that she does all year. My older sister is still talking about it. I'm fasting, but I think I'm still going to try to make it out here."

"It's just down the block for me," I say, gesturing out our window in the vague direction of my house. "Our shul is right next door, so I won't be far. It's my first fast." I'm not twelve yet, the age when girls officially start fasting, but I'm close enough that I'm determined to try to make it through Yom Kippur without eating or drinking. "I'm hoping I can handle it."

To my surprise, it's one of Tzivia's friends who speaks up, after only a sidelong glance at me. "You have to get a giant Gatorade beforehand," Temima tells us conspiratorially. "Drink the whole thing the morning before Yom Kippur and you'll barely notice that you're fasting. My whole family does it."

I make a face, but I'm relieved that Temima is talking to me. "I hate Gatorade."

"It's not so bad when it's cold," Temima says. "Except last year, when they were all sold out except for the yellow ones. They were *awful.*" She wrinkles her nose. "Glad I didn't need to fast last year. My older brother already picked up a dozen blue ones this time."

Tzivia laughs and responds, and I do too, distracted from the stares around the classroom and heartened by how Temima chats with me. When recess is over, I have something to cling to, even if it's just that Tzivia and her friends might actually talk to me after vacation.

At dismissal, I gather my project in my arms and wait at my desk, hoping to avoid talking to anyone else at the end of the day. Tammy and Sheva walk past me, and Tammy says, "Your project looks nice." It's a little snide, and I can feel the weight of it fall on my shoulders.

"I didn't ruin your projects," I say, and I leave it at that. I won't take the blame for things I haven't done.

Tammy looks back at me curiously, and then they're gone too.

I walk out of the class once I'm sure the hallway has emptied, the last few girls loitering near their lockers and not mine, and I collect my things and head downstairs. I can do this. I can handle being the class pariah.

If I keep telling myself that, I might believe it someday.

CHAPTER **23**

The weekend is quiet. Shabbos Shuva, we call this Shabbos. The Shabbos to return to our best selves and start fresh. There are speeches all afternoon, and even Bayla goes to one. I beg my way out of them, unwilling to spend my afternoon in a class. "I'll go to Morah Neuman's Yom Kippur event," I promise Ema. "I just need a break."

"One day back in school and she's already sick of it," Bayla says wryly, but she leaves me alone. We've been closer since my suspension, and we spend most of Shabbos on the couch together, playing card games and passing magazine articles back and forth between us. Bayla is disappointed that Gayil hasn't exposed her involvement in the pranks. "It's what she deserves," she says. "She's just going to stand by and let you take the blame?"

"I thought you didn't want me sending my letters," I protest. "Now you wanted me to?"

"No," Bayla says, shaking her head. "I wanted you to be the bigger person. I just also wanted her punished." She smiles a deadly smile, like an alligator right before it charges. "Her time will come."

I sigh. "I'd rather just put it all behind me," I admit. "It's done. It was stupid. I learned my lesson." I can't stop myself from peering out my window though, looking for some sign of Gayil across the lawn. After Shabbos, I see that there's a little Post-it in the corner of the window, a smiley face drawn on it in permanent marker. I don't think that it's directed at me, so I ignore it.

Yom Kippur is Monday night, and it's a very different holiday than Rosh Hashanah. We spend most of the day in shul on Rosh Hashanah, but the prayers are less tense, less laden with the weight of all our mistakes of the year. There are no big meals like the four that we have on Rosh Hashanah. Instead, everyone fasts. I try Temima's Gatorade tip and it works. By midday, I'm tired and hungry but I can still easily walk down the street, past little kids playing by themselves on their lawns and older girls drooping on their porches.

I don't know if I'm really going to go to Morah Neuman's event at the end of the day. I'm filled with dread at the idea of returning to school, even for this, and experiencing the cold shoulder from my classmates all over again. This is going to hang over me for a lot longer than just vacation, a mark against me when there had never really been marks for me at all. Am I just inviting more resentment today, even during Yom Kippur?

As the sky begins to get dark, the end of Yom Kippur creeping in, my head is starting to pound from the fasting. I go to our shul, next door to Fairview Bais Yaakov, and I hover at the door, uncertain of where to go. Ahead, I can leave all my regrets behind for a little longer, and I won't have to face anyone I've hurt. But to the left is a chance—to do something, maybe, and make a tiny difference in what happens next.

I hesitate, and someone says, "Shaindy? Is that you?" It's Rena, eyeing me with misgiving, and I twist around.

"We daven here," I say in explanation. "I was just...going back in."

Rena frowns. "Morah Neuman's thing is starting soon. You're not going?" It isn't an invitation—why in the *world* would Rena want me to accompany her—but I hesitate, and I take a wavering step toward her. She waits for me, her head tilted as she takes me in, and she doesn't move again until I'm beside her. "I think it'll be nice," she says. "I have a neighbor who had Morah Neuman last year, and she said that it was *healing*—like we have all that much to heal from in sixth grade," she adds wryly. "Like, my hair got slime in it. It wasn't like I was thrown in a van and driven cross-country."

Maybe it is something about the stillness of Yom Kippur. Tonight, with the sun setting around us and the sounds of prayer drifting through the air, there are no kids rolling up and down the streets, no toddlers in the park or cars trying futilely to make it past hordes of children. I have never seen Fairview so immersed in silence, and it lends itself to reflection. "I am *so* sorry," I blurt out. "You had the prettiest hair, and I . . ." *Gayil*, but not just Gayil. I had watched it all unfold and had been a willing accomplice.

Rena looks at me. She doesn't shrug off the apology like Tzivia had, only seems to examine me as though to search for sincerity. And when she gets it, she nods abruptly. "Yeah," she says. "You did." Not forgiveness, but acceptance. I feel weak and grateful for it.

We walk another few steps, rounding the corner to the entrance to Bais Yaakov, and Rena says, "Was it Gayil?"

I stop short. Rena stops with me, her eyes unsmiling, and I stare at her silently. Rena says, "I know she's been upset with me, but I don't know why. And I keep thinking about you almost coming over to us in the supermarket, and . . ." She exhales, low and weary, as though it takes far too much energy to express. "Gayil and I had plans on the first day of Rosh Hashanah. But when I got there, her sister told me that she was at your house. I didn't even know that you were friends."

"We're not," I say, and I am mostly sure of that. I don't want to lie, not on Yom Kippur, but I don't want to create the kind of rift that is creeping up around us. I clear my throat. "But you're her best friend," I murmur, and I mean it. "And I'm sure that she wouldn't keep something like that from you. Not forever."

I wait. I'm terrified of giving anything else away, and so I stand there, swaying a little in the heady weakness of the end of the fast. Rena takes my arm, and she walks me to the door, her hand steady. "Come on, Shaindy," she says. "Just another forty-five minutes."

The classroom is the only room on the floor that is lit, the dark hallways bringing me back to my nights with Gayil. The same peace that I'd felt outside seems to have seeped into the classroom too, and the girls who are already there are silent, drifting off in their desks or watching the door tiredly. Fasting on Yom Kippur heightens the intensity of the day, and we're all close to falling down from a high.

This is our last chance to hold on to it. Out of twenty-six girls, fifteen are here. Tzivia has her head on her desk, and Temima is doing her best to sniffle quietly. Devorah greets Rena with a wan smile, and Sheva is still davening from her siddur, turning pages quickly.

Gayil is here too. I stare at her. I have built her up in my mind over the past few weeks—as the model to aspire to, as the perfect friend, as an evil mastermind—and it is strange how the clarity of Yom Kippur lets me see her exactly as she is: just a girl, complicated and angry, and afraid of being forgotten. Just like me.

Maybe not just like me. I see the way that Rena nods to me, the way that Gayil stares at Rena in surprise, and I wonder at how her gaze shifts to unguarded longing when Rena can't see. Maybe I do have something that even Gayil doesn't have: a clean slate. The pranks no longer hang over me, not like they do over Gayil's head. I have nothing to hide anymore.

I'm still watching Gayil when Morah Neuman comes into the room, and we spring to our feet out of respect, stumbling a little with the end-of-fast exhaustion as we do. "Sit," Morah Neuman says, putting up a hand. There is a tremble to hers from her fast, a crack in her voice that makes her just a bit less commanding.

She sits too, on top of her desk with her hands splayed against the hard brown wood. "We talk a lot about teshuva," she says. "But it's hard to grasp, until now, exactly how difficult it is. You've been in shul all day. Most of you have fasted. But we don't do these things to punish ourselves. We do them to reflect, and I'm sure that you have reflected."

She clears her voice. "The hardest thing that many of you will do in your lives—harder than almost anything else you might experience—is admitting that you were wrong. We make mistakes, and then we make them a part of ourselves. We are built of other people's hurt," she says, and her words have never felt so true. "And to apologize—to take back that piece of ourselves—it can feel impossible."

Sheva has finished davening. Devorah is watching Morah Neuman, her head drifting up and down in a nod. Morah Neuman says, "We're going to take a first step tonight. Not apologize," she clarifies. "That's not what this is about. I want you each to find someone in this class you've hurt. Maybe not in words that you're ready to express. Maybe it was just a spiteful thought, or excluding someone unconsciously, or something that is better off left unsaid. And all I want you to do is to look into each other's eyes."

It feels insurmountable now, with my head heavy from fasting and prayers, from how late it is and how tired I am, to think back through the past, to figure out who it is that I want to apologize to. There are the obvious choices, Gayil's five targets, but I don't want my Yom Kippur to be only about that. Not when there is a whole year to mull over.

I stand slowly, and then I stop. A girl is in front of me. *Devorah.* She holds my gaze, and I wonder what it is that she's ever done to me. Devorah is genuine, is popular for being no-nonsense and kind, and I hate the idea that she's ever thought something spiteful about me.

But her eyes are warm, regretful, and when she moves away, I find it in myself to move. I stand in front of Rena, who nods silently to me in grudging acceptance. I move to a few other girls, and there are strange apologies that pass between our gazes, regrets that aren't verbalized but I still understand. We are letting go of something here, old hurts and exclusions, and it is easier than ever to look Sheva in the eye, to meet Sari's eyes, to meet Tammy's.

Everyone else mills around the room, finding their own partners. There are a few sidelong glances at me, but no one else comes to me. No one is ready to fully forgive yet, though they must wonder about Devorah and Rena's willingness to catch my gaze. It isn't something I will explain to them. I'm relieved that no one seeks that explanation.

Morah Neuman says, "One more minute," and then, someone is in front of me. *Gayil.* We hold each other's gazes, and I don't know what I see in her eyes. It isn't an apology. I don't know if Gayil is ever going to shed those pieces of herself that she has tacked on with every prank and attack. They make up a hard shell, a furious protection that Gayil clings to even now, and I only feel compassion for her. I smile tentatively, and Gayil only stares, a hand falling onto my arm.

She lets go, and Morah Neuman says, "I think it's time we went downstairs."

The shul in the auditorium is full, benches crowded with women and girls on our side of the curtain, and we sway with them and lose ourselves in that final prayer of Yom Kippur as it begins. I close my eyes, press my fist to my chest and recite the alphabetical confessional of vidui, word by word. *We are guilty. We have betrayed.* The words are in Hebrew, but I run through them in English in my head, feeling the weight of them against me with my fist.

Yom Kippur ends with the sound of a shofar, ringing out like a horn through the auditorium, and I am dizzy with hunger and overwhelmed at the experience when it's over. The mood shatters in an instant, the stillness gone as my class chatters with each other about their fast and about Morah Neuman's exercise. It's as though the past day had never happened, and I look around uncertainly, positive that I'm about to get iced out again. Meira darts a nervous glance at me. Chana Leah whispers something to Temima. I close my eyes, already resigned to it, and I slip out of the auditorium, hurrying home.

I'm not the only one who leaves quickly. Gayil makes her exit just as I do, walking swiftly through the street back to the development as I take the sidewalk. Around us, the sleepy silence of the past day is fading. Adults hurry back from shul to break their fasts, and kids ride scooters through the streets again. The silence is gone, and in its place is laughter and relief, recovery from an ordeal that we have put ourselves through as a community.

And, keeping time with me down into the development, is Gayil. She walks sure and true, and an onlooker might only see a confident girl, another child of Fairview who thinks she owns the street. Only someone who knows Gayil well will understand the power that she holds. The fury that, when unleashed, can make her into someone larger than life, someone who could change the world if she wanted it.

Once, I'd wanted to drown in that strength. Today, I glance over at Gayil and I don't know what I want from her anymore.

She steals glances at me too. The street is alive with people, but we look only at each other as we hurry home. The world has narrowed down to the two of us, walking in perfect time ten feet apart, the weight of the past few weeks still lingering between us. Yom Kippur can't heal every wound, but it all feels less sharp now, on the verge of something stronger.

I reach my house a moment after Gayil reaches hers, and I turn to walk up the path as Gayil reaches her porch. By the time I make it to my porch, Gayil should be inside.

But when I look up, there she is: staring at me from her porch, her face unreadable. "Hey, Shaindy," she says.

I start, then stare back at her. "Hi." I'm not sure what I expect from her now. Maybe a reminder that we're even, or a threat if I say anything to her friends. Maybe just a snide comment.

But she surprises me, as Gayil always can. "My sisters and I cooked up a *storm* to break the fast," she says. "Muffins and potatoes and eggs and pasta. It's the best meal of the *year*." She tries to smile, though it emerges uncertain. "Want to come over and eat with us?"

"Why," I say blankly. I don't know if this is a trap, or if this is an apology. I can't imagine Gayil managing an apology.

Gayil shrugs. "It's going to be our year, Shaindy," she says, and she sounds so strangely tentative, like someone I've never met before. "Come on over."

I think about it. I try to imagine it, being Gayil's friend. *Belonging*, and living in the light that Gayil casts with her attention. It's a dream that I would have latched on to in an instant in another lifetime—one in which I'd never looked up one day and found a girl holding a sign at her window and inviting me into her inner circle.

I could be so happy.

I could be that girl again, the one who'd done terrible things in the name of friendship. It would be so easy to fall back into it, to do anything to gain Gayil's approval and affection. And I don't know. I miss that girl a little bit. I miss *Gayil*. But I don't think that Gayil's friendship is my end goal anymore.

I smile at her. It feels odd on my face, this compassion, and I feel more like Tzivia in this moment than myself. There are worse people to be. "I don't think that's a good idea," I say, and Gayil looks startled, then embarrassed.

I don't want that either, not anymore. I clear my throat. "Hey," I say, and I'm the one who sounds strong now. "I'll see you in school, yeah?"

Gayil's humiliation fades, and she nods grudgingly. "Yeah," she says. "I'll see you then."

We walk into our houses. I'm the first one home from shul, and so I put the soup on the stove, then run upstairs to my room. I just need to take care of one thing before I set the table, something I haven't done in years. It's a silly little thing, but it's always lingered, waiting for a moment I've been craving for longer than I could express it.

The moment has come and gone, and it's time that I step back from it and see what else I can be beside Gayil's.

I pull down the window shade that looks out on Gayil's window, and I go downstairs to greet my family.

Acknowledgment

I am so immeasurably grateful to the people who have made this book a reality. To my gifted editor, Arthur A. Levine, who has made all my dreams come true twice now, and with such enthusiasm and faith in a story that I don't think could have been told anywhere else.

I'm fortunate to work with a publisher as passionate and inclusive as Levine Querido, and I must personally thank the people who worked directly on Shaindy: Madelyn McZeal, Antonio Gonzalez Cerna, Irene Vázquez, Kerry Taylor; and Arely Guzman, who has been efficient and a great sport throughout. Thanks also to Michelle Margolis, who gave the book a thoughtful sensitivity read. The cover of this book was created by the talented Jenna Stempel-Lobell, who went above and beyond—I'm still in awe at the lettering, and I adored all the options you offered us!

Tamar Rydzinski is the best agent anyone could ask for, and I'm so glad to have her guiding me through every step of writing and publishing (and for a ride home in the rain, that one time!).

This was a book casually conceived on my parents' couch one Shabbos evening, the setting decided after a second Shabbos in my sister's development. Tova, Ema, thank you for being my most enthusiastic readers and supporters! Thank you too to the rest of my equally enthusiastic family: Abba, Ma and Pa, Shira, Ora, and the Yons. I have wonderful friends who have been steadfast in their support as well: Batsheva, Maia, Ariella (also family!), Luisa, Sharon, Bracha, Eve, and too many others to name, though they know exactly who they are.

Finally, this book and every single thing I write is only possible because of Moshe Meir's unending support and frankly baffling level of tolerance for my idiosyncrasies. And much love for my peanut gallery as well: Yishai (still waiting on a book about *boys*), Ayala (quietly scribbling better stories in her own notebooks), Akiva (bastion of five-year-old-caliber imaginative and mildly alarming creativity), and Zahava (very disappointed at my attempt to make any part of my existence not about her). Y'all make writing around you a delight.